In the final second before Ashley pressed her lips to his, she closed her eyes.

Sensation sizzled through her, but not just from sexual chemistry. The knowledge that she and Rick fit made her bold, curious. What would it be like to be involved with a man who didn't hesitate to teach her, to consider her an equal, to love her for real, not just for her money?

Putting her hands on Rick's shoulder, Ashley stepped closer, deepening the kiss.

Dear Reader,

July might be a month for kicking back and spending time with family at outdoor barbecues, beach cottages and family reunions. But it's an especially busy month for the romance industry as we prepare for our annual conference. This is a time in which the romance authors gather to hone their skills at workshops, share their experiences and recognize the year's best books. Of course, to me, this month's selection in Silhouette Romance represents some of the best elements of the genre.

Cara Colter concludes her poignant A FATHER'S WISH trilogy this month with *Priceless Gifts* (#1822). Accustomed to people loving her for her beauty and wealth, the young heiress is caught off guard when her dutiful bodyguard sees beyond her facade…and gives *her* a most precious gift. Judy Christenberry never disappoints, and *The Bride's Best Man* (#1823) will delight loyal readers as a pretend dating scheme goes deliciously awry. Susan Meier continues THE CUPID CAMPAIGN with *One Man and a Baby,* (#1824) in which adversaries unite to raise a motherless child. Finally, Holly Jacobs concludes the month with *Here with Me* (#1825). A heroine who thought she craved the quiet life finds her life invaded by her suddenly meddlesome parents and a man she's never forgotten and his adorable toddler.

Be sure to return next month when Susan Meier concludes her CUPID CAMPAIGN trilogy and reader-favorite Patricia Thayer returns to the line to launch the exciting new BRIDES OF BELLA LUCIA miniseries.

Happy reading!

Ann Leslie Tuttle
Associate Senior Editor

Please address questions and book requests to:
Silhouette Reader Service
U.S.: 3010 Walden Ave., P.O. Box 1325, Buffalo, NY 14269
Canadian: P.O. Box 609, Fort Erie, Ont. L2A 5X3

One Man
and a Baby

SUSAN
MEIER

*The
Cupid
Campaign*

SILHOUETTE *Romance*®

Published by Silhouette Books

America's Publisher of Contemporary Romance

For my brothers and sisters and friends.
If you hadn't endured hours of phone conversations
and encouraged me, I wouldn't be here today.

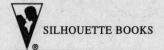 SILHOUETTE BOOKS

ISBN-13: 978-0-373-19824-5
ISBN-10:   0-373-19824-8

ONE MAN AND A BABY

Copyright © 2006 by Linda Susan Meier

This edition published by arrangement with Harlequin Books S.A.

® and TM are trademarks of Harlequin Books S.A., used under license. Trademarks indicated with ® are registered in the United States Patent and Trademark Office, the Canadian Trade Marks Office and in other countries.

Visit Silhouette Books at www.eHarlequin.com

Printed in U.S.A.

Books by Susan Meier

Silhouette Romance

SUSAN MEIER

is one of eleven children, and though she's yet to write a book about a big family, many of her books explore the dynamics of "unusual" family situations, such as large work "families," bosses who behave like overprotective fathers or "sister" bonds created between friends. Because she has more than twenty nieces and nephews, children also are always popping up in her stories. Many of the funny scenes in her books are based on experiences raising her own children or interacting with her nieces and nephews. She was born and raised in western Pennsylvania and continues to live in Pennsylvania.

Dear Reader,

This second installment of *The Cupid Campaign* has bad boy Rick Capriotti meeting his match in Ashley Meljac. Competing for the same job, they set out to exploit each other's weaknesses. Instead, they find an incredible attraction that seems all wrong but just won't go away.

Ashley was a great character to create and explore because she's a strong, determined woman. Taken for half of her inheritance once before, Ashley has something to prove. And if she falls for Rick, she'll become a laughingstock.

But Rick is handsome, sexy and the best kisser on the planet. He's also got a secret tucked away that he'll defend at all costs….

It's a fun book about serious subjects that made me laugh and cry as I was writing. I hope you enjoy reading it as much as I enjoyed writing it!

Susan Meier

Chapter One

"If you want the job as manager of Seven Hills Horse Farm, it's yours."

Standing in the doorway of her father's office, Ashley Meljac gaped in horror as her dad offered *her* job to a man in a black T-shirt and tight-fitting jeans that were molded to a very well shaped backside. She'd asked for the job four years ago and her father had refused because she'd just come home after losing half her trust fund to an opportunist she had married, but he'd promised that she'd get her shot someday. Since then she'd more than proven she'd learned from her marriage mistake and she wasn't letting her dad off the hook of his promise.

"What are you doing!"

His green eyes wide with surprise, Gene Meljac sprang from his seat behind the heavy mahogany desk.

Wearing jeans and a T-shirt, he was dressed almost the same as the man with his back to her, but compared to the tall man in the black jeans, Ashley's dad looked short and stout.

"Princess! I thought you weren't home."

"Well, I am," Ashley said, striding across the mustard-colored Oriental rug beneath the tan leather sofa and chair in front of her dad's desk.

"Ashley, this is Rick Capriotti," her dad said hastily. "Rick, this is my daughter, Ashley."

Stetson in hand, Rick Capriotti politely faced her. His black hair casually fell to his forehead and brushed his shirt collar as if he'd forgotten his last trim. His blue eyes were so pretty they seemed almost too feminine in a face with chiseled cheekbones and a slightly crooked nose.

Those intense blue eyes caught her gaze. "Your daughter and I already know each other."

Ashley took a breath, ignoring the sexual sparkle in his beautiful eyes. She wasn't one of the legions of Calhoun Corners co-eds who had spent their high school years giggling after the mayor's two bad-boy, heart-throb sons. She only knew Rick because she had been the freshman assigned to tutor him so he could pass American Literature in his senior year. He'd expected her to fall at his feet with hero worship and ghostwrite his midterm paper and any other papers he needed for the class. She'd insisted on actually teaching him. So he'd asked for and gotten another tutor, but from that day on he'd harassed her and teased her every chance he got.

Yeah, she was thrilled to see him.

Especially since *she* wanted the job that he had been offered and she intended to get it.

She faced her dad again. "Why are you giving him my job?"

"I'm not *giving* him your job," her father assured her as he scrambled around his desk to catch her hands. "I'm hiring Rick to run things during my vacation. I'm taking more sailing lessons, remember? Advanced lessons that require the commitment of some real time. I won't be home until February."

Ashley said nothing, still smarting over the fact that her father had chosen to spend Christmas away from her. She knew he was head-over-heels in love with sailing, but he was breaking the pact they had made to always spend holidays together. When he'd told her about the trip and she'd reminded him of their pact, he'd told her that he hadn't forgotten the sleepless snowy night right after her mother and brother were killed when he'd promised she'd never be alone. He simply felt they were both beyond the grief, and they should be moving on with their lives.

She'd retreated then, telling him it was fine for him to spend the holiday sailing. She'd have plenty to do. She wouldn't, but she also wouldn't tell him that on a lost bet. She didn't think he'd understand that buried in his argument for moving on was the fact that his plans clearly didn't include her. That hurt just a little too much. So she'd consoled herself with the knowledge that someday she'd run this farm, and that being intimately involved in the process and with the people would make it even more her home, but now it appeared he was breaking that promise, too.

"Besides, Mr. Capriotti isn't looking for permanent employment. He just needs a job for a few months while he considers his options."

As her father turned to walk back to the chair behind his desk, Ashley flicked a glance at the man in question and just barely held back a snort of disbelief. Right. She wouldn't believe anything Rick Capriotti said. He hadn't been just a kid who smashed mailboxes and deflowered virgins like his brother, Jericho. Rick was a finagler. When his dad took away Jericho's car as punishment, Rick was the one who got the class nerd Eric Brown a date with a cheerleader in exchange for the use of Eric's wheels. Rick was the one who sweet-talked two girls into providing alibis for him and his brother when the distributor caps went missing from all the high school buses before the first day of class in Jericho's senior year. Rick was the one who talked teachers into grading on a curve and talked himself out of detention. More than that, though, despite the fact that his family hadn't been wealthy back when Rick and Jericho were in high school, Rick had never, ever been without money.

Rick was somebody who figured all the angles and got exactly what he wanted when he wanted it. Now that Ashley thought about it, he was Calhoun Corners's equivalent to her scheming ex-husband. Which meant she *really* did not want him anywhere near her family's fortune.

"But you told me that I could take over the farm," she said, grabbing her father's forearm to stop him before he reached his chair.

"I said *someday* you could take over the farm. Not today. You're not ready."

"How do you know? You've never given me a chance—"

"You're an accountant?"

At the deep-voiced comment from the man she was trying to ignore, Ashley quietly said, "This is none of your concern."

"I'm sorry," Rick said, so polite Ashley wanted to shake him. "But it is my concern. A lot of people who live on farms like this one don't realize the behind-the-scenes work that goes into keeping them afloat."

She glared at him. "I studied business in college."

"But you've never used those skills," her father reminded her gently. "And Rick's right. You haven't seen half the behind-the-scenes work. You ride, you care for your own horse and you might even talk shop with Toby, but you don't know the intricacies that go into keeping this farm successful."

"Because you haven't shown me!"

"And now I'm leaving," her father said, as if she'd just made his argument. "And Mr. Capriotti will handle things."

Turning away from Ashley, Gene put his hand on Rick's shoulder. "Let's introduce you around this morning. Then you can jump right in tomorrow."

"Tomorrow!" Ashley gasped.

"Yes, I leave tonight."

"I thought you were leaving next week! When did your plans change? And why didn't you tell me?"

"Sweetheart, my plans just changed yesterday."

Ashley's chest tightened. His plans had changed the day before? Twenty-four long hours ago. He could have told her last night or at breakfast. Yet he hadn't. Since his last visit to the Bahamas, he'd been consumed with sailing. With him giving up control of the farm, not caring that he spent the holidays away, and forgetting to even mention his change of plans, Ashley had to concede that he wasn't "moving" on; he'd already "moved" on.

Which made her all the more determined that she wouldn't lose control of the farm. If she had nothing else in her life, at least she'd have the farm to keep her busy and give her a sense of home.

"I'm sorry," she apologized because she had to get this situation in hand and she had to do it now. "I know how excited you are about sailing. But that's all the more reason for you to teach me how to run the farm."

Her dad smiled. "You really want to learn to run the farm?"

"Yes."

"Great!" Gene shifted his gaze to Rick. "So, Mr. Capriotti, it looks like you just got yourself another assignment while I'm gone. My daughter here wants to learn the ropes and since I'll be away, that means you're the guy who gets to teach her."

Ashley gasped. "What?"

Rick's voice sounded confused. "What?"

"It's perfect. Ashley really did take enough accounting and business courses to be able to manage the farm. After three months of you explaining the technicalities and putting her through the paces, and me working with her for three or four months after that, she could take over next summer when I sail around the world."

Ashley swallowed. "Sail around the world?"

"Yes. I hadn't made concrete plans yet, but that's always been my ultimate goal. And now that everything seems to be falling into place here, I can put this thing in motion." He headed for the door. "Before I give Rick the tour of the farm, I'm going to run upstairs and grab my cell phone." He faced Rick. "I'll just be a minute."

With that he walked out of the den and absolute silence reigned. Ashley was so stunned she couldn't have spoken if she wanted to. Rick Capriotti had no trouble finding his voice.

"Congratulations, Ms. American Literature Tutor, it looks like the tables have officially turned for us."

At seven o'clock that night, tired and furious, Rick jerked his extended cab pickup to a stop in front of his sister Tia's house. After a hectic day of not only being shown around Seven Hills Horse Farm and meeting hands, but also being reminded every thirty seconds of things he would need to teach Ashley, Rick's nerves were strung so tightly that he worried he'd snap.

He didn't like the idea of having to show the ropes to the woman who he remembered as being a spoiled rich girl too snotty to do him a favor back in high school. He liked even less that he'd continually noticed that she had grown up rather nicely. All day his attention had been snagged by the way the sun glimmered off her pretty yellow hair. Or the way her green eyes seemed to catch fire when she held back her anger. Or the way the jeans she'd put on to tag along on Rick's tour of the farm made her look tall and sexy. The whole time he was supposed to be remembering names of employees and details of the farm, he was noticing *her*. And he didn't even *like* her. Hell, he didn't *want* to like her.

Frustrated, he ran his hands down his face. He needed a shower and a beer. Too bad he wasn't going to get either for at least two hours.

Jumping out of his truck, Rick glanced at the neat and proper French Colonial house before him. His sister Tia and her new husband, Drew, who had been a neighbor of the Capriotti family for more than ten years, were expecting their first child, so she was doing most of her work as an advertising consultant from home. Knowing how busy she was, he'd hated to impose on her to babysit his six-month-old daughter, but when he, Tia and his mother sat down to figure out his dilemma, it was Tia who suggested he leave Ruthie with her.

He jogged up the three steps of the wood plank front porch to the entryway. Before he could knock, Tia opened the door, holding Ruthie on her arm. Tia had dressed the baby in lime-green one-piece pajamas and tied a white ribbon bow on the wisp of nearly black hair on the top of her head. That little bit of feminine fussing combined with the way Ruthie's blue eyes sparkled, sent a tremor of guilt through Rick. He did not know how to care for a baby. He was lucky to get Ruthie through the day with the basics. He never thought of the nice things Tia did as second nature. His poor daughter had really drawn a losing number in life's parent lottery.

Reaching for Ruthie, he said, "I can't begin to thank you, Tia, for babysitting her."

His dark-haired, blue-eyed sister laughed. "Rick, this

is my pleasure. Not only is Ruthie the most adorable baby I've ever seen, but also I need the practice." She smoothed her hand along her stomach, which still looked fairly flat to Rick, but he knew better than to say anything. Tia was thrilled to be pregnant and ready to shout it from rooftops. She wanted to be showing.

"Besides, my caring for Ruthie here at the farm, away from prying eyes in town, is the perfect way for us to keep her a secret until you figure out how you want to handle this."

Tia motioned for Rick to follow her into the foyer, then down the hall to the gray, yellow and beige kitchen. As Tia began packing the baby's rattles and plush animal toys into the diaper bag, which sat on one of the kitchen chairs of the oak table in the breakfast nook, Rick said, "I just don't like the idea that we even have to keep her a secret from Dad."

"It can't be helped. Dad's already nervous because it's the first time in over a decade that he has an opponent in the mayoral election. If we tell him about Ruthie, especially that she's Senator Paul Martin's granddaughter, he won't be able to hold a conversation without Mark Fegan knowing something's wrong," she said referring to the editor of the *Calhoun Corners Chronicle* who supported her dad's opponent, Auggie Malloy.

"You'll be the most logical reason for Dad's extra nervousness, since your being home is the new thing in Dad's life. I'm guessing Mark will assign his daughter Rayne to investigate and with her experience on the Baltimore newspaper she'll easily uncover that you spent four years on and off running with Senator Martin's daughter. And once Rayne finds Jen Martin, she'll find Ruthie."

Rick shook his head. "I don't think so. Jen lived with her mother in Europe while she was pregnant and had Ruthie there. No other paper has picked up on it."

"Maybe not. But what if Rayne does? What do you think her instincts will tell her to do if she discovers that while Senator Paul Martin, high-profile member of the board of directors for Americans for Morals, was preaching family and commitment in his latest campaign, his daughter abandoned her child to a guy most noted for being a rodeo bum?"

Not insulted by Tia's description because it was accurate, Rick knew exactly what Rayne would do. She would sell the story to a national newspaper or magazine. Then Rick would be in big trouble. There was only one way for a man who made a career out of being a staunch supporter of family to counter his own daughter abandoning a child: rescue the child from her disreputable parents and raise the child himself.

Rick kissed Ruthie's cheek. There was no way on God's green earth he was going to let that happen. Not only did he love Ruthie, but Jen had told Rick a thing or two about Senator Martin after seeing her dad posturing on television one day. The most revealing of which was that he'd forced her mother to sign a nondisclosure agreement when they divorced because he had been physically abusive toward both Jen and her mother. Jen had had no reason to lie, and Rick couldn't think why the senator would want a nondisclosure agreement unless he'd done things in the marriage that he couldn't afford to have revealed. That also explained why Jen's mom found it necessary to move halfway around the world to be away from him. She was afraid of him.

It wouldn't be the first time a politician lived a double life. And, truth be told, Rick didn't give a damn if Senator Martin preached one thing and practiced another, as long as he didn't try to get custody of Rick's baby.

"If you think this through," Rick said, as his sister continued to gather toys and stuff them into the navy-blue quilted diaper bag, "there's really no reason for me to ever tell anybody who Ruthie's mother is."

Tia shrugged. "For now. As long as nobody goes digging, you may never even have to bring up who Ruthie's mother is. But you're eventually going to have to tell Ruthie."

"Not really. I was toying with the idea of telling Ruthie that her mom is dead."

Tia grimaced, as she continued to gather Ruthie's things. "I don't know, Rick. I think that might come back to burn you. Jen could change. She could suddenly grow up and want to see her little girl and then she will look like the mom desperately trying to have a relationship with her daughter and you'll look like the dad who lied."

Knowing that was true, Rick said nothing.

Zipping the diaper bag closed, Tia said, "You don't have to make any decisions today, Rick. You have two whole weeks until the election."

"You mean two long weeks to hide her."

"Yes, but once the election is over your secret will be safe. Whether dad's reelected or not, Rayne will lose interest in him and have no reason to check into your life."

"Except that she's just plain mean."

Tia laughed. "Hey, stop worrying. Until all this is settled, between Mom and me, you'll always have a babysitter. And since you don't get off work until after dark, it's not as if you have to sneak Ruthie into the Meljac's guesthouse. If you think about it, technically, we're not even really keeping Ruthie a secret. We simply aren't announcing her."

Tia walked to the refrigerator. "I made some more formula," she said, changing the subject as she slid the bottles into the side compartment of the diaper bag. "I also went online and found a pediatrician for you. Since I was already surfing the net I read up on what and how much she's supposed to eat and I discovered it is okay for her to be eating the rice cereal that her mother had put in the diaper bag she left with you."

Rick smiled and nodded, glad he'd done the right thing by guessing Jen had been feeding Ruthie the cereal since a box had been packed with her things. But inside he was anything but happy. When Jen had showed up at his door with Ruthie, he'd thought she'd come back to him because she loved him. He'd foolishly thought that becoming a mother had caused her to see how right they were for each other and that it was time for them to be a family. He remembered how joy had flooded him. He had loved her with ever fiber of his being and when she had left him the year before it had damned near killed him. So, when she suddenly appeared that night, all he could think of was being grateful for a second chance.

After Jen put Ruthie to sleep, they'd made love and he had been the happiest man alive. It had never occurred to him that she was conning him, suckering him into believing everything was fine so he wouldn't suspect that she intended to sneak out in the middle of the night. Nothing had surprised him more than when he awakened to find himself alone with the baby. Her note had actually threatened a lawsuit if he told anyone she was Ruthie's mom. She had so casually, calculatedly left him and their baby that anything he felt for her died an instant death.

Now, all he wanted was to raise his baby in peace. As long as Jen kept Ruthie a secret and Rick kept Ruthie a secret there was no reason for her dad to find their baby and get involved. And that was exactly what Rick wanted. Privacy.

"All packed," Tia announced, helping him hook the strap of the diaper bag on his left shoulder since Ruthie was nestled against his right. "I'll see you in the morning. At four or so."

He grimaced. "I'm really sorry about this."

"Hey, it's not a problem. Drew gets up when you do, so I do, too. Besides, as I said, I need the practice."

Rick smiled his thanks and left his sister's house. Ten minutes later he pulled his pickup in front of the guesthouse for Seven Hills Farms. Ruthie pounded her rattle on her car seat, which he had strapped onto the backseat of his extended cab, and Rick turned around.

"Didn't we talk about this?"

She cooed and gurgled and Rick shook his head, then shoved his way out of his truck and opened the back door that gave him access to Ruthie. She slapped his nose with her rattle.

"Didn't Daddy tell you that you have to keep down the noise?"

She tilted her head in question, as he lifted her from the car seat. Perching her on his left arm, he reached inside to loop his fingers through the strap of the diaper bag and yanked it out.

Making his way up the steps of the small porch to the front door, he glanced around at the little Cape Cod house, thinking how perfect it was for him and Ruthie. There were two bedrooms on the second floor, so they could sleep in the same general area and he could hear her when she cried in the middle of the night. Gene had shown him a cozy green kitchen filled with appliances, a living room furnished with a comfortable overstuffed sofa and chairs and a den where he could put his computer and network into the farm's system to do the books. Best of all, it was far enough away from the farmhouse that no one could see or hear what he did. A side road veered off Seven Hills's main access route and brought him to the secluded guesthouse. He didn't even have to pass the Meljac residence to get home.

That was another thing that had fallen into place with this job. Being so far away from the main house, there was no danger Ashley Meljac would discover Ruthie. It was clear from their meeting that morning that Ashley would like nothing better than to be rid of him. But he wasn't going anywhere. Gene Meljac hadn't precisely said that he was retiring, but he was showing all the signs. This time next month Gene could call, find everything running smoothly without him and realize he didn't need to run the farm anymore. Then this job with the perfect house, far enough out of civilization where a man really could keep a secret, would be his.

He wasn't letting some born-to-shop Paris Hilton wannabe run him off. Especially since he was absolutely positive that once she saw the real work of managing a farm she'd turn up her nose and hightail it to the nearest mall.

In fact, now that Rick thought about it, by this time tomorrow he intended to have proven to Princess Ashley that she didn't really want to run a farm at all.

Chapter Two

Rick only had to open three doors in the convoluted maze of halls in the upstairs of Gene Meljac's sprawling home before he found Ashley's bedroom.

He flicked a switch as he stepped inside, lighting the two lamps on her bedside tables. Those, unfortunately, illuminated a ten-foot-tall tufted white leather headboard that led to yard after yard of crinkled pink material that looped around to create a canopy. A pink rosebud bedspread covered the small lump he assumed was Ashley. At least twenty pillows of varying shapes and sizes—and shades of pink—were scattered about on the bed to cushion her every move.

He shook his head. Wow. He'd certainly pegged this one right.

"Come on, princess," he said, grabbing the thick rosebud comforter and yanking it off.

He instantly regretted that. The sight that greeted him took his breath away, and he couldn't stop his gaze from traveling from Ashley's pink-tipped toes, up her bare long legs, to the pink fur-trimmed hem of her tiny pink nightgown with some kind of top that looked like a fur-trimmed bra.

He sucked in some air. He should have left the cover on. But it was too late now.

"Come on," he said, grabbing her foot to pull her off the bed but she was so silky soft he couldn't get a grip. His hand slid from her heel to her toe and she giggled.

"Stop that!" She nestled into her pillow. "And come back to bed."

Rick's mouth fell open in shock, but his libido instantly decided joining her was a fabulous idea. He nearly slapped himself for even considering it. Never in a million years would he again be interested in another woman accustomed to creature comforts. Ashley might not be so spoiled as to abandon a child in favor of trips to the Mediterranean the way Jen had, but she was obviously pampered. All he had to do was look at the multiple doors on the right-hand wall. They undoubtedly led to a closet, dressing room and private bath, most likely with a spa. This suite was bigger than any bedroom in his parents' home. Hell, this suite was bigger than any apartment he'd lived in since he'd struck out on his own. He didn't want anything to do with another woman who needed an entire room for her clothes.

"Get up!" he yelled, resisting the urge to smack her butt to get her moving. "You want to run the farm, fine.

Then I'll teach you to run the farm. But that means you have to get up!"

She shifted on the rosebud sheets. "What?"

"Today's the day you start learning to run the farm, remember?"

Her eyes popped open. She bolted up in bed, saw him, glanced down at herself and screamed.

"No one's here," he said frantically searching the room until he found a frothy see-through pink thing that he assumed was the "cover-up" to her little pink nightie. He scooped it up and as he released it to toss it to her, the pink fur tickled his palm. His blood began to hum through his veins. Wild thoughts scampered through his brain. Luckily he was smart enough to ignore all of it.

"So screaming won't do any good. Besides, I'm here to get you for work, not for what you apparently offered somebody last night." He shook his head. "I'll bet you have some dreams in that getup."

She snatched her cover-up in midair. "My dreams are none of your concern."

"Except your dream about running this farm." He crossed his arms on his chest. No matter what his per-colating hormones thought, he didn't intend to deviate from his plan to get rid of her. Not even for the various and sundry fun and games that automatically sprang to mind just looking at that nightgown.

"Now get up."

She tied the belt of the pointless robe. "In case you haven't noticed, I *am* up."

He looked at his watch. "Great. And only twenty minutes after everybody else is in the barn."

She gaped at him. "What?"

"What do you think? Horses sleep until noon? Fat chance. Kiss your late nights goodbye, sweetheart."

She drew a breath. "If farm managers have to get up at—" she peered at the digital clock on her bedside table "—four-thirty! Are you insane?" She jumped out of bed and stormed over to him.

Rick forced his eyes away from her legs only to find himself staring at her breasts, then the long column of her neck, then her blazing green eyes.

"I'll get up at five."

"All rightie, then. When your dad calls I'll tell him you must not want to learn because you refuse to get up when everybody else does." He turned and strode toward her bedroom door.

"You wouldn't!"

He faced her again. "I would. You think a farm is a big game?" he asked, motioning around the room. "With your pretty pink foo-foo stuff all over the place? But most of us live and die by whether or not this farm makes money and while I'm here, it will." With that he pivoted toward the door again. "You're in the barn in ten minutes or I'll be telling your dad."

He left the room and Ashley fumed. Not because he threatened her but because he'd had the audacity to come into her room. She ripped off her cover-up as she marched into her walk-in closet and searched for a pair of jeans suitable for a day in the barn.

He hadn't merely come into her room, he'd come in and pulled off her covers. She glanced down at her basically see-through nightgown and groaned. It would probably take less than five minutes for her fetish for pretty nighties to get around the barn. She'd just handed Rick Capriotti the ammunition he needed to keep her from gaining the respect of the hands.

Damn! This was not at all how she had pictured this morning would turn out. She hadn't exactly seen herself arriving at the barn, shaking hands with Rick and giving everyone in the barn a pep talk. She hadn't even imagined herself and Rick Capriotti getting along. But she had envisioned some sort of compromise. This farm was her home and her heritage and she wanted to run it with the grace and dignity of a well-bred Southern lady. But right at this very minute, Rick Capriotti was probably robbing her of that chance by telling everyone she wore a little pink nightie trimmed in fur that made her look like one of Santa's off-season elves.

She took a breath, told herself not to panic and decided the only way to handle the gossip would be to meet it head-on. That was the lesson she'd learned when she came home after her marriage crumbled. For four long weeks every room she had walked into had suddenly gotten quiet. Then she had realized that if she would talk about her disastrous marriage, admit she lost half her trust fund and answer any questions, eventually the gossip would die, if only because the townspeople would have nothing to speculate about. They would know everything.

So, she'd spilled her guts to Ellen Johnson, wife of the diner owner, who usually acted as hostess, and it worked like a charm. Within a week, everybody knew her story, and bored because there were no unanswered questions, they moved on to the next gossip topic.

And that was exactly how she'd handle the nightie scandal. She would address it head-on.

Ten minutes later she was in the main barn, striding down the cement aisle that separated the two long rows of stalls. When she stepped into the office, Rick glanced at her, looked at his watch, then smiled. "You had thirty seconds to spare."

Not about to be baited, she returned his smile. "I didn't shower."

"Most of us don't before a day of mucking stalls."

Her pretty smile collapsed. "Mucking stalls!"

"What? You think you're going to start at the top?"

"I am the top! I own this farm."

"Let's get something straight. Your dad owns the farm or I wouldn't be here and you wouldn't be putting up with me."

Toby Ford walked into the office, carrying the morning paper and a cup of store-bought coffee, and wearing a flat tweed cap that made him look like the epitome of the English gentleman that he was. Though he was close to forty, his boyish face and rakish charm reminded Ashley of someone her own age.

"Morning, Miz Meljac," he said, taking off his hat, and not meeting her gaze. From his awkwardness Ashley guessed Toby was the first person Rick had told about her nightgown, and the place she'd have to start with damage control.

She straightened her shoulders. "No need to be so

formal, Toby, since it's clear you probably know more about me this morning than you knew this time yesterday."

Toby peeked at her. "Excuse me?"

"Oh come on, now. If we're all going to work together, we might as well be honest."

"About what?" Toby's eyes widened.

Ashley glanced from Toby to Rick, who was smirking, and then back to Toby again. "He didn't tell you anything…about…well, this morning?"

"I just got here," Toby replied at the same time that Rick said, "A gentleman doesn't tell what he sees in a lady's bedroom."

Ashley's eyes narrowed.

This time when she spoke she had to ungrit her teeth. "Mr. Capriotti felt it was okay to come into my bedroom to wake me this morning."

Leaning back on the old-fashioned wooden office chair that sat behind the gunmetal-gray desk, Rick linked his hands behind his neck. "Let me ask you something, Toby. If you had a laborer who wasn't on time for work, what would you do?"

Toby shrugged. "Fire him."

"My point exactly." Rick turned his gaze on Ashley. "So you had a choice, sunshine. Get your butt down to this barn or get fired. Since I suspected you didn't know that rule, I did you a favor by waking you."

He rose. "Let's go get you set up to do some mucking."

"Mucking?" Toby gasped.

"Sure." Rick smiled at Toby. "Isn't that how you started most hands when they came to that big farm you ran in England?"

"Well, yes."

"But I'm not really *starting* here," Ashley said, turning her smile on Toby. "Right, Toby? I've been around my whole life."

"Yet, you've never mucked a stall," Rick said.

She took a breath. "No. But I'm fairly certain I have the principle down pat."

"You probably do," Rick agreed. "But if you really want to become the boss over people who have been here for the decades you were only *riding* the horses they cared for, you have to let them see that you don't think you're better than they are. That you understand what it's like to work."

She held his gaze. More than anything else she wanted her workers' respect. They would become like family to her, if only because they would be the people she spent the most time with. She needed what Rick was offering her. The chance to prove she believed they were all equal. Family.

He was right. She had to do this.

"Let's go."

Ashley wasn't in the shower until six o'clock that night. The hot water that sluiced over her was like a soothing balm to muscles that ached from the strain of manual labor.

She pressed her face into the steady stream of hot water. Even her cheeks were tired. Her hair smelled like manure. Her legs were so overworked that her thighs quivered. Her hands had blisters.

She looked down and tears filled her eyes. Her hands

had blisters. Real blisters. No matter how much she had enjoyed the camaraderie of the farmhands with whom she worked, she couldn't muck stalls again tomorrow. Not unless she wanted to get blisters on top of her blisters and she did not. Somehow or another she had to get out of mucking tomorrow without giving the employees the impression she thought she was better than they were. Because if she couldn't she might as well quit...

She squeezed her eyes shut and groaned. *That* was what Rick wanted. He wanted her to quit! It made sense that he would be trying to get her to give up before she was trained so that when her dad came home in February he'd be the only one in the running for *her* job.

With water sluicing over from her hair to her neck and aching shoulders, she realized that even if it wasn't Rick's intention to get her to quit, he would still win when her dad came home. If he kept her mucking stalls instead of involved in what she needed to learn, he would remain the better choice to run the farm when her dad's fixation with sailing turned into full-blown retirement next summer. Because she knew it would. She'd already accepted that her dad had moved on. Officially retiring was just the next step. He might come home in February after this three-month sailing excursion, but when he did, she suspected it would only be to pick a replacement.

And that meant there was no way she could let Rick win.

She stepped out of the shower, toweled off, blew her hair dry and brushed her teeth. But instead of sliding into the pair of pink silk pajamas—long pants and a shirt in case Rick decided to wake her again—that she'd laid out on the bed, she marched to her dresser and grabbed a pair of jeans and a clean chambray shirt. She pulled on socks and boots and even got out one of her old cowboy hats, deciding that it couldn't hurt to look the part of the job she wanted, then she ran downstairs and out the back door to her SUV.

It was only about a quarter mile to the guesthouse. On a day when her legs weren't still rubbery from exertion, she probably would have walked. But in order to assure that she didn't crumble on Rick's doorstep, Ashley drove, pulling her SUV beside his extended cab pickup, then dragging herself up the three steps to the wood plank porch.

A screen door protected the open front door of the living room. The glow from one of the end table lamps provided enough light that she could see no one was on the floral sofa. There appeared to be a lot of "stuff" on the floor, but nobody around.

She glanced down the hall and noticed the kitchen light was on and decided somebody had to be inside. Mustering energy she absolutely didn't have, she lifted her hand to the door and rapped twice.

No one answered.

"Rick?" she called through the open screen.

No answer.

She knew he was in there. Only an idiot left a house with so many lights on. She frowned. Or maybe he was on the back porch?

Not about to walk down the three porch steps, around the front of the house to the side and down the length of the house to get to the back porch on her shaky, achy legs, she opened the door, stepped into the living room and nearly tripped over a little chair.

She peered down at it and frowned. It looked like a baby seat of some sort. One of those carrier things? Maybe a car seat?

Confused, she stooped down to examine it more closely and two seconds later she heard the sound of feet pounding down the steps. She glanced up to see Rick frozen about midway on the staircase.

Their gazes caught and held. The shadow of beard on his chin and cheeks said he hadn't yet had time to shave, but his clean jeans and shirt, and slicked-back wet hair said he'd showered.

"I thought this house was mine, for my use."

Ashley took a breath and rose. "It is. I'm sorry. I saw the lights and assumed you were home."

He finished his walk down the stairs. "If you've come here to tell me that you're done playing farmhand," he said, scooping up the chair Ashley was now positive was some sort of baby chair and tossing it behind the overstuffed green sofa in the corner of the room. "Then I'm okay with you just walking into my house. If not—"

"If not what?" she asked, her eyes narrowing. "I seem to remember you coming straight into my bedroom this morning, without my permission, when there were no lights on…oh, and, in a house you don't own."

His face hardened. "You might own this one, princess, but you assigned it to me. It's just like a rental. You can't come in without my permission."

"And you can't come into my bedroom without my permission."

He crossed his arms on his chest. "So, I guess we'll just call it even?"

She smiled and strolled over to the floral sofa. "I don't think so," she said, pulling the baby seat from behind it. "What's this?"

He didn't say anything.

She held it up to inspect it. "I'm not a genius. I'm not even a woman who's particularly familiar with babies, but I'm guessing *this* belongs to a baby."

He still said nothing.

"And if you didn't have a baby around here some-where, right now you'd be saying something. Anything. Like maybe, yeah, it's a baby seat. I bought it for my sister Tia for when her baby is born."

"It's a baby carrier. I bought it for my sister Tia."

She smiled. "Too late. Too, too, late." She took a breath, glanced at the seat again. "So where is she?"

"She?"

"I know it's a girl." She pulled a tiny hair clip from a fold in the plastic padding of seat. "There's no way in hell you'd put one of these on a boy."

"She's upstairs."

Ashley's aching muscles all but cheered with relief. "So, you and I are about to start a little bargain-ing session."

"I don't think so."

"Oh, I do. The very fact that you slid this chair behind the sofa like I was some sort of ninny who would forget she saw it if you got it out of my sight, proves that you're hiding your child." She paused, tilted her head. "It is *your* child, right?"

He said nothing.

"You know," she said, walking around Rick as if he were a thoroughbred at an auction. "I'm not that good at ferreting out information, but I bet if I called Rayne Fegan and I told her you had a baby in here, she could figure it all out."

"Don't."

"So we are bargaining."

"What do you want?"

"I don't want to have to muck out stalls."

"Your job can't be on the table."

"My job is the only thing I want on the table!"

"Forget it. If you really do get to be manager of Seven Hills, the people who work for you have to see you don't think you're above them."

"Nice try, but one day of sweating and making friends with the staff got that point across. If you keep me mucking any longer I'll know you're just doing it so you don't have to teach me the things I need to know."

He shook his head in disgust. "Your dad told me he wanted you trained. Putting you through the paces is my first responsibility, whether you like what I do or not. If you really want to lead, you have to understand the people who work for you, how tired they get so you can balance their workloads."

"So you weren't avoiding training me?"

"No. What I was really doing was throwing you into the fire. If anything I expected you to accuse me of trying to get you to quit."

Her eyes narrowed. That *had* crossed her mind. "Were you trying to get me to quit?"

"I don't think there's any trying about it. If you're not cut out for the job, the work will force you out on its own."

"If I hadn't found this bargaining chip it might have."

He said nothing and Ashley laughed. "I've got you and it's really fun." She tilted her head, thinking, then added, "The only thing I can't figure out is why you need to hide a baby."

"Because my dad's election is in two weeks and Ruthie's mother abandoned her. I don't want my mistake to hurt my dad's campaign."

"Not buying it. Even if your baby's illegitimate, single parent babies aren't really big news anymore. Your having a baby wouldn't hurt your dad's election."

Rick said nothing and Ashley sighed. "Okay. Here's the deal. I don't want you gone. I need you to teach me. But I can't have you hiding at Seven Hills if you kidnapped that baby or something. You have to come clean with me."

When Rick again didn't answer, Ashley shook her head in disgust. "I guess this means you're leaving."

"I'm not leaving. Your dad hired me to do a job and I intend to do it."

"Then I'm back to asking Rayne Fegan to look for the truth."

"Can't you just let this alone?"

"No, for all I know you've got Britney Spears's baby in my guest house. I cannot let this alone. If you won't leave, or tell me the truth, I'll have no choice but to call Rayne."

He drew in a ragged breath. "Ruthie's mother is Senator Paul Martin's daughter."

"Oh!" Ashley said, picturing the gorgeous young woman who loved to get her face in the paper, flaunting her lifestyle to embarrass her popular, well-loved, conservative dad. "You and Jen Martin were…" She stopped and stared at Rick.

His face hardened. "Can't see her with somebody like me?"

Quite the contrary. Ashley could easily see what Jen Martin saw in Rick. He was sexy. No. He wasn't just sexy. He dripped sex appeal. Piercing blue eyes. Rippling muscles from real work, not hours at a gym. An attitude that all but screamed trouble. Yeah. She knew exactly what Jen saw in Rick. She just couldn't quite see what Rick had seen in Jen.

"You tell Rayne I have a baby and it will take her about ten minutes to discover that Senator Martin's daughter not only had a baby that she kept secret, but she also abandoned her. Then it won't be me or Jen who suffers, it will be my daughter whose face will be splattered on front pages all over the country by people trying to unseat Senator Martin."

Knowing he was right, and that this situation was more complicated than just a bargaining chip in their fight for a job, Ashley paced away from him. But before she could say anything, a cry issued from upstairs.

She turned in time to see Rick pivot and vault up the steps, as if it were the most natural thing in the world. He took the stairs two at a time and disappeared around a corner, crooning, "It's okay, Ruthie, Daddy's here."

The affection in his voice was like a shot to Ashley's heart. A man couldn't fake the kind of emotion she'd heard in that one short sentence. Curious beyond words, she tiptoed up to the second floor but stopped short of the door. Peeking around the door frame, she saw Rick cradling a small bundle in pink pajamas.

The little girl sobbed pitifully, not comforted by being cradled. Rick shifted her to his shoulder, putting her tiny face in Ashley's view. Pretty blue eyes, just like Rick's, blinked back at Ashley, then the baby quit crying.

At the same time Rick turned. When he saw Ashley, he sighed. "It's you."

"I'm not leaving until we straighten this out."

He shook his head. "That's not it. I thought she had stopped crying because I'd comforted her. Now, I know she only quit because a woman came into the room."

Ashley smiled. "She likes me?"

"Don't get too carried away. She's very curious about women. Probably because she had one in her life and doesn't now."

Studying the baby who was about the prettiest thing Ashley had ever seen with her black hair and big blue eyes, Ashley was again struck by the emotion for the baby she heard in Rick's voice. She knew most fathers put their children first, but it seemed odd to see Rick Capriotti do it. He'd already admitted he was protecting her from being used as a pawn by people trying to destroy her grandfather's career. Now, he was worried about her missing her mom. His behavior was so different from what Ashley expected, she couldn't even address it. She wouldn't know how.

"Can I hold her?"

Rick reluctantly said, "Sure."

Ashley took the little girl and her mouth automatically tipped into a smile. "Well, hello," she said, holding the baby an arm's length away so she could look at her. Then she peered over the baby's shoulder to Rick. "What's her name?"

"Ruthie."

"That's right. Ruthie." She smiled at the baby. "Hello, Ruthie."

Ruthie gurgled.

Rick laughed. "She usually yelps at me."

The note of pleasure in his voice caused Ashley's heart to do another flip-flop. His obvious love of the little girl and his honest wish to win her love was incredibly attractive. Luckily Ashley hadn't been one of his high school groupies or right now she'd probably be swooning.

"You're her source. Yelping is how she tells you she needs something. Besides, you know the old saying. You always yelp at the one you love the best."

Ruthie giggled.

Ashley grinned at the baby, then peeked at Rick. "Do you think she understood that?"

Rick bent to pick up a bear and two dolls that were on the floor in front of the small white crib. "I think babies are a hell of a lot smarter than we give them credit for being."

"She looks like you."

"Thank God," Rick said, then he grimaced. "Jen didn't exactly leave me with a lasting good impression of her. I'd prefer not to see her face every time I look at Ruthie. More than that, though, I don't want Ruthie to see the mother who abandoned her every time she looks in the mirror."

Again his stark honesty hit Ashley right in the heart. He'd been hurt and couldn't hide it, but more than that he understood that his daughter would suffer when she realized her mother hadn't wanted her and that hurt him, too.

That almost brought her to tears and she had to admit something she'd never thought she would. Rick Capriotti had changed. Really changed. Worse, when she added his new personality to his good looks, he suddenly became very attractive to her. With his black hair drying in ringlets, the day's growth of dark whiskers shadowing his chin and his shirt pulled out of his jeans, he looked sexily disheveled. Like a man who needed to be kissed, then fed dinner.

Ashley brought that thought to a swift halt. Being attracted to Rick Capriotti was a normal gut-level reaction, but the deal about kissing him and making him dinner was just insane.

She settled the baby on her shoulder. "Okay. I'll keep your secret." She paced the floor, rocking the baby in a move that suddenly felt very natural. But as quickly as she realized that, she also figured out what was going on. Her dad leaving had made her long for family and Rick and his little girl were a ready-made family. An adorable baby and a sexy man were a deadly combination for a woman whose only real desire in life was to have a home. Intellectually she knew getting attached to this baby or this baby's daddy was ridiculous. But, emotionally, it was second nature. An honest need coming face-to-face with two people who could fill that need. Her brain wouldn't overrule her emotions on this one. Especially not if her hormones got involved. Best to get the hell out of here!

"I'm not keeping the secret for you. I'm doing it for Ruthie. But that doesn't mean I'm going to roll over and play dead so you get the job as foreman of my dad's farm permanently."

She turned and handed Rick's baby to him, then locked her gaze with his sexy blue eyes. A frisson of awareness danced along her skin. And she knew it was officially too late. If her hormones hadn't been engaged before this, they were now.

"This job is mine."

And she was getting the hell out of this room before the man currently at her mercy realized she had a weakness, too...

Him.

Chapter Three

He couldn't let her leave with her last words hanging in the air. She knew his secret, and allowing her to have the last word could give her a false sense that she had the upper hand. She didn't. Despite her promise not to tell, he was still the boss. It would be a betrayal of Gene's trust in him if he allowed Ashley to take control when she was nowhere near ready. Not only that, he didn't intend to lose this job. It was perfect for him: a quiet farm where he could keep his daughter out of everybody's line of vision.

He laid the now-sleeping baby in the crib, then stepped into the hall, closing Ruthie's door behind him. "Don't think you've got me running scared."

Ashley stopped dead in her tracks in the hallway, pivoted and stared at him. "I'm doing you a favor and you snap at me?"

"You're only paying back the favor I did for you this morning."

"I would have preferred that you explained that situation to Toby this morning. I wanted the air cleared," she said, but her voice shivered oddly and Rick frowned. Surely she wasn't afraid of him. "I wanted the truth out. Unlike you, I don't keep secrets."

She turned to run down the steps, but again Rick couldn't let her go. It was one thing for her to fear him as her boss. Quite another for her to be "afraid" of him.

He stopped her by grabbing her wrist, and her gaze leaped to his. Her pretty green eyes widened and she shivered, and it was all Rick could do to keep from laughing out loud. She wasn't *afraid* of him. She was *attracted* to him. That was why she was running. She wanted to get away before he noticed, but it was too late.

"I get the distinct impression that you might have a secret or two."

To her credit she held his gaze. "I don't."

Rick ignored her words and focused on her feathery, breathless voice. He skimmed his index finger over her wrist and was rewarded when her breathing stuttered.

"I could kiss you right now and you wouldn't run."

"Not until after I'd kicked you."

He laughed and leaned forward just a bit. She didn't move. Didn't shrink back. If nothing else, the kid had backbone.

"But you'd like it."

"So would you."

This time it was his breath that froze in his chest. The hell of it was she was right. Staring into her fiery green eyes, feeling her soft skin against his palm, he couldn't deny it. He would enjoy kissing her, so for that very reason he stepped back.

"Go home. We have a busy day tomorrow."

She turned and headed for the steps.

Just to make sure they were clear about their situation, Rick added, "Don't think your job will be any easier because you know about Ruthie. As far as I'm concerned we're even."

Halfway down the steps she turned again. "You came into my bedroom. I came into your house. That's even. But not the part about the baby secret. You owe me on that one."

"And I'm paying you back by keeping the secret that you're attracted to me. So once again, we're even."

She shook her head with disgust and started down the steps. But Rick knew two things. First, she hadn't seen that he'd reacted to her, too, or she would have had a snappy comeback. Second, she had gotten his message. They both knew she was attracted to him and they both knew that was enough to keep her in line at least until she grew accustomed to it.

Marching up the sidewalk to the hardware store the next morning, Ashley didn't even let herself think about how she looked—or smelled. She knew what was going on. Rick might not be the finagler he was in his misspent youth, but they were in competition for a job and sending her into town was an easy way to embarrass her and clearly illustrate that if she got this job this would be her life. A sweaty, smelly farmworker. Dressed in the oldest clothes she could find in her drawers. Her hair matted into ringlets from sweat. No makeup.

But contrary to what Rick expected, she refused to be embarrassed. Not just because she wouldn't let him win, but because she accepted that this *was* her life now. She wanted to be the farm manager. She wanted to care for the horses, dicker for new mares, negotiate the sale of foals, hire hands, settle small battles, maintain the property. She wanted to be connected to the land and the people of her small town as one of them. No longer an outsider, or her father's daughter, but one of them.

She pushed open the hardware store door and the bell rang, alerting Bert Minor to her arrival. "Hey, Bert," she called striding down the aisle. "I'm here to pick up the part Rick ordered this morning."

The tall, round, hardware store owner scrambled out of the back room, drying his hands in a brown paper towel. "Hey, Ashley. How's it going?"

"It's going great, but apparently Rick or somebody needs some part and I was elected to pick it up."

He looked pointedly at her oversize gray T-shirt and threadbare jeans, apparently not realizing that in some parts of the world she'd be in style.

"They must all be super busy."

"*We* are super busy," she said, emphasizing the "we" so Bert would start thinking of her as one of the workers, not just a resident of the farm. "That's why I didn't have time to change clothes. Besides, you might as well get used to me looking like this. Right now I'm learning as much as I can about running the place, and when my father retires I hope to be the one who takes over."

He smiled approvingly. People in Calhoun Corners weren't fond of outsiders and they liked it when a farm passed from one generation to the next. "Yeah. Your dad told me he was retiring."

Though Ashley had suspected her father would probably officially retire when he returned in February, hearing that he'd already announced it in town froze her breath in her lungs. Still, she schooled her features, not so much to prevent Bert from seeing that it hurt her to hear it from him but so that he wouldn't guess that her dad seemed to be telling everybody but her.

"He called the day before he left to go sailing and put Rick's names on all your accounts," Bert said, examining the screen of his computerized checkout system, subtly alerting her to the fact that everybody knew Rick was in the running for the manager job, and to him it looked as if Rick was in the lead.

She only smiled.

"So, you don't have to sign for this or anything." He handed her a brown bag that held something heavy. "Just don't drop it."

"Right."

"And good luck with learning the ropes. I'm pulling for you."

"Thanks." She walked out of the hardware store and directly to her black SUV. She carefully set whatever the hell was in the bag on the floor in front of the passenger's seat, then slammed the door closed. Rounding the hood, she passed the dress shop and stopped suddenly.

Janie Alberter was running her fall sale, but Ashley's attention wasn't caught by something pretty for herself.

What stopped her dead in her tracks was the little sundress the shade of Ruthie's eyes.

It was the cutest thing Ashley had ever seen and without any trouble at all she could picture Rick's little girl wearing it. Not only that, but buying the dress was exactly the kind of gesture she wanted to show Rick that she was handling this, not just the work, but the transition from normal woman to normal woman *and* farmhand, and doing it without hard feelings. She refused to give him any sort of opening to tell her dad she was a whiner. She didn't want to give him anything but positive feedback to report to her dad.

She clicked the button on her key chain that locked her SUV and strode into the dress shop.

"Janie," she said walking up to the counter. "I want that little blue dress that's in the window."

Janie turned and faced Ashley. To her credit she didn't say a word about Ashley's unkempt appearance and acted as if she didn't notice, probably because Ashley was her best customer. "The baby dress?"

Ashley nodded.

"Why would you want a baby dress? Who do *you* know that has a baby?"

Ashley held back a groan. For someone who had promised to keep Rick's little girl a secret, Ashley had just made a huge mistake.

To cover it she smiled and said, "A friend of mine had a baby a few months ago and I bought a gift at the time, but I just love that little dress so much that I'm going to send that along, too."

"Well, aren't you sweet," Janie crooned. "Give me

two seconds to get it into a bag." She started walking away, but turned and said, "What size?"

"Size?"

Obviously having been through this before, Janie smiled. "How old is she?"

"I'm not sure."

"Is she this big," Janie asked, spreading her hands about a foot-and-a-half apart. "Or this big?" she asked, moving her hands about six inches further away. "Or this big?"

"The second one."

"Okay, we'll say six months."

Knowing Rick was waiting for his part, when Ashley returned to Seven Hills she immediately lifted out the brown bag, leaving the baby dress behind, and delivered it to Rick who only grunted.

Not quite sure what to do, Ashley stayed in front of the old metal desk until he glanced up.

"What? You want applause?"

"No, I was sort of hoping I could grab some lunch before I go back to the stalls."

Looking down at the paperwork he had been review-ing, Rick dismissed her saying, "Fine."

Determined to be the most chipper, happy farmhand Rick Capriotti had ever seen, Ashley said, "Thanks, boss," turned and headed up to her house. She entered through the back door and walked past the oak cabinets, brick-red colored walls, copper pots and American Southwest print rugs on her way to the laundry room and first floor bath. She took off her clothes, depositing them into the washer, and then showered. If only because she couldn't imagine eating a sandwich smelling the way she did.

Stepping out of the shower, she grabbed the bath towel she'd brought in from the laundry room, then padded upstairs to her bedroom. She dressed in another pair of old jeans and a T-shirt, then grabbed a stack of clean jeans, T-shirts and underwear and ran down the steps. After storing the fresh clothes in the bathroom for future use, she ate a sandwich with a glass of iced tea, then strode down to the barn again.

Completely forgetting about Ruthie's dress she went back to work, lifting and pushing and otherwise disposing of smelly straw until her back ached. Once again, it was six o'clock before she left the barn. Once again, she thought she might have to crawl up the steps to the back porch and then across the kitchen floor to the first floor laundry room and bath.

Hot shower water again took away a good bit of her muscle aches. Cocooned in a clean bath towel, she walked up the steps to her room and into the section of her dressing room that contained her nightgowns. She reached for a pretty blue one with spaghetti straps— something so pretty it would make her forget the now-broken blisters on her palms—and suddenly remembered the sundress she had bought for Ruthie.

Deciding that there was no time like the present to give Rick her peace offering, she blow-dried her hair, slid into a pair of capris and a three-quarter-length sleeve white blouse and drove down to the guesthouse again. This time she waited until Rick answered her knock rather than entering on her own.

Wearing a fresh T-shirt and jeans, with his wet hair combed off his face, Rick appeared at the screen door holding Ruthie, looking clean and so wholesome Ashley stared at him mutely. Every damn day the man got more handsome.

"What do you want now?" he asked through the door, which he kept noticeably closed.

Ashley presented the bag. "I saw this in the store today when I went to pick up the part for the main mower."

For some reason or another his pretty blue eyes narrowed into slits.

"You went shopping when I sent you into town for something for the farm?"

"No!" she said, suddenly understanding his annoyance and glad she had a good explanation. "I saw this," she said, thrusting the package at the door again, "as I was walking to my car."

He still didn't open the screen door.

"What is it?"

"It's something for Ruthie. A dress."

His eyes that had been little blue slits suddenly widened and filled with fire. "What?"

"It's a dress. A pretty dress."

"She doesn't need another dress."

"Of course, she does," Ashley said with a laugh. "No girl alive has enough clothes."

Rick turned away from her and marched into the living room where he set the baby in her portable chair. Assuming she was invited in by default, Ashley opened the screen door and stepped inside. She pulled the dress out of the bag and displayed it.

"See? It's the color of her eyes."

He turned so quickly that Ashley gasped.

Eyes burning into her, he said, "Let me make this perfectly clear. I don't want your charity. Worse, if you think this dress is a bribe to get me to lighten up on you, you just made the biggest mistake of your life. I don't need anyone buying clothes for my child."

Ashley gaped at him. "This was neither charity nor a bribe," she said, infuriated at his tone. "I bought it because it's pretty. And she is pretty. And she and the dress match perfectly."

Rick stepped even closer to Ashley, coming so near only a breath of space separated them. She could see the white-hot anger in his eyes, feel the heat radiating from him. But instead of being afraid, Ashley felt her body responding to his nearness. Her fingers itched to touch him. Her blood percolated through her veins. Her breathing became erratic.

"Not a bribe?" he asked softly.

She licked her lips. "No."

"Because if you wanted to bribe me, you have much better temptations at your disposal."

He only ran one finger across her chin, but Ashley felt the touch the whole way to her toes.

"I'm not here to bribe you…"

"Oh come on. I've lived at Seven Hills for three nights. You've visited me on two of them. I guessed last night that you were attracted to me. Now, you're bringing me a present. I know the signs, honey. I know exactly what you're doing. Remember I dated somebody like you."

"Yeah, well, I dated somebody like you, too," Ashley said, furious with her traitorous body for being covered with chills and wanting to melt against him. Hadn't she already learned this lesson? "He took half my trust fund. I wouldn't be interested in you on a lost bet."

"Oh I get it. You're here because you're *not* interested."

Ashley could handle the backbreaking labor required to strengthen her body to be physically able to do the job she wanted. She could handle changing her life—changing even the entire town's perception of her. But there was no reason to put up with personal abuse. Rick Capriotti might be the world's most gorgeous man. He might even be a nice guy with his baby. But she didn't want anything to do with him. No matter what her traitorous hormones thought.

She tossed the dress onto the chair. "Think what you want. But the dress isn't a bribe. It's a gift. And it's not even a gift to you. It's a gift to Ruthie. If your pride can't handle somebody buying clothes for your child, I will respect that and I won't buy anything else. But since I already bought the damned thing you're stuck with it. Rest assured I won't make another nice gesture for you again."

Ashley pounded out of Rick's living room, down the porch steps and to her car. Rick heard the roar of her SUV engine when she gunned it, spewing gravel as she drove away, and he cursed. Ashley Meljac was going to be the death of him.

He walked though his downstairs turning off lights, gathered Ruthie and then wearily climbed the stairs and went to bed, knowing he should have handled that better and not quite sure why he hadn't. But it all became crystal clear the next morning when he couldn't stop yawning as he drove to the diner for coffee after dropping Ruthie at Tia's.

Exhaustion had him too weak to be as sharp as he needed to be. Though most nights he went to sleep before ten, Ruthie woke him at least once. Then he was up at four to get her fed and over to Tia's, so he could be in the barn at four-thirty. It was no wonder he'd over-reacted to Ashley's gift and let his attraction to her get the best of him.

Though exhaustion was a good explanation, it didn't solve the problem. At least not completely. Rick was sure Ashley wouldn't ever buy another gift, but he and Ashley were always going to be attracted. He knew all about male/female chemistry. And the kind he and Ashley shared was the kind that didn't go away without at least a little experimentation. That's what made their attraction trouble. Neither one of them would forget about it until one of them did something to scratch the itch, and it wasn't going to be him. He'd learned his lesson about socialites. They didn't think long-term when it came to cowboys. Cowboys weren't mate material. They were the objects of flings. They were for a good time. They were for a little fun. But after the fun, they were yesterday's trash.

Frowning, Rick pulled into a parking space in front of the diner, wondering if that would really be so bad. Not the part about being trash, but the part about the fling. The mistake he had made with Jen was falling in love. If he went into an affair with Ashley knowing their relationship would end so he couldn't get too attached, he wouldn't get hurt. And as long as he let her be the one to break it off, she wouldn't get hurt, either. They could both get the attraction out of their systems, and get on with the business of working together.

"Good morning, Rick!" Ellen Johnson, wife of Bill Johnson who owned the diner, greeted Rick as he pushed open the glass door. Twenty or so wooden tables were scattered about and a long shiny red counter matched the booths that circled the outside rim of the room. Red and white checkered curtains hung on the wall of windows beside the booths.

"Hey, Ellen, just coffee."

Standing behind the cash register at the end of the counter, tall, brown-haired Ellen smiled. "To go?"

"Isn't it always."

"Yep." She turned and reached for the coffeepot with her right hand as she retrieved a takeout cup with her left. "So how's it going at the Meljacs's?"

"Fine."

"I hear Ashley's working, too."

He couldn't help smiling. The gossip mill in this town was swift and efficient. "Yep."

"I'm glad."

Because her back was to him, Rick rolled his eyes.

"She's really had a rough life, you know," Ellen continued as she handed Rick his coffee and returned to the cash register. "First her mom and brother dying in that auto accident."

Rick nodded. He wasn't in Calhoun Corners when her mother and brother were killed, but he hadn't been home a day before he'd heard about it.

"Then that *boy* she married, stealing half her trust fund."

Rick handed Ellen a twenty for his coffee. "She was married?"

"A whole year. Got married at twenty. Got divorced at twenty-one. And lost her fight to keep her trust fund at twenty-two."

Ellen took a breath before she set Rick's change on his open palm. "Let me tell you something, Rick. Ashley's really toughened up after everything she's been through, but the gossip nearly killed her."

Considering that Ellen was currently the one telling the tale, Rick only smiled.

"I wouldn't want to see her go through another bout like that."

"If she learned her lessons she probably won't."

"I would say you were right except now with her daddy leaving, she's probably vulnerable."

Not quite comfortable with the direction the conversation was taking, Rick said, "I suspect she is."

"So she might look like an easy mark to somebody with a little more experience."

At that Rick's spine straightened and he hissed out a breath. He got it now. Ellen was warning him off. He almost couldn't believe it, then wondered what he expected. The people of this town had always thought the worst of him. He'd given them cause when he was a teenager, but no one had stopped to consider that he might have grown up.

"You know, Ellen, that's very interesting. But I learned a whole bunch of things myself, so I know a bit about mistakes. If Ashley really learned her lessons as you say she did, then she shouldn't have anything to worry about."

He left before Ellen had a chance to reply, and cursed a blue streak driving back to Seven Hills. He hated people like Ellen who spent their days talking about other people, but he hated even worse that she was right. He and Ashley couldn't even have a fling. The gossip would kill them. In every whispered scenario, she'd be a stupid idiot for hooking up with another opportunist and he'd be the opportunist.

The fling idea absolutely wouldn't work to settle their attraction, which meant he was back to his original conclusion. The one he made the very first night he stayed at Seven Hills. His only option was to get rid of Ashley. But this time it wasn't just to keep his job. It was to prevent both of them from becoming the object of gossip. If he didn't get her to stop playing farmhand somebody would notice the look in her eyes when he walked in her direction, or the twitch of Rick's palm when she was close enough to touch, or hear the quiver in either one of their voices. Then the gossip would be so bad they'd both have to leave town.

And he couldn't do that. He needed the security and privacy of a place like Seven Hills and he needed this job. More than that, if everything Ellen said was true, then Ashley needed to be with her dad. She needed to drop the idea of running the family horse farm and move to the Caribbean.

Rick pulled his truck into a parking space in front of the barn, got out and strode into the office. When Toby arrived fifteen minutes later, coffee in one hand, newspaper in the other, he fell onto the seat in front of the desk. "You get your coffee?"

"Got some at the diner."

Toby shook his head. "One cup of coffee is hardly enough to get the old engine started." He handed his store-bought cup across the desk. "You can have this one."

"I got mine to go." Rick lifted his takeout coffee.

"Saw you driving over to your sister's this morning, too."

"Yeah, thought I'd stop by and say hello."

Toby laughed. "At four o'clock in the morning?"

"You more than anybody else know about the odd hours a manager has to keep. Since Drew gets up before dawn like I do, it's as good a time as any to visit."

Accepting that, Toby nodded. "Your sister's a good girl."

"Yes, she is," Rick agreed. He didn't know what he'd do if she hadn't been available to help him.

"And Ashley's a good girl, too."

Rick glanced up. He'd wondered why Toby was suddenly so full of small talk this morning. Now he knew. Rick was about to be slapped with another sermon. But at least he could reason with Toby. Maybe even win him over to his side.

"Yeah, Ashley might be a good girl, but she doesn't belong running a farm. Hell, she doesn't even belong working here. She should just go back to riding and doing whatever else it is girls like her do."

"I think you're wrong," Toby said, then sipped his coffee. "I can see her chatting up potential buyers for the horses or sweet-talking the guys we want to buy from."

"I don't need to sweet-talk anybody. I can negotiate well enough on my own without any extra assets."

"I'm just saying that it never hurts to have a secret weapon."

"I know all about secret weapons, Toby. I dated somebody like Ashley and let me tell you secret weapons get old fast. And sometimes they even backfire."

To his surprise Toby laughed. "Yeah, I suppose there are times when that's true. Gene's been trying to get old man Clemmons's farm from his boys for the past six months. First time out, he went over there with candy for the kids and all kinds of gifts and the Clemmons acted like he was there to trick them out of their land and all but called the chief of police."

Picturing it, Rick laughed.

Toby shifted on his seat. "Yeah, we're laughing, but it wasn't funny then. Gene was amazed he even got them to sign a preliminary agreement."

"What's holding up a final agreement?"

"What else? Money."

Rick nodded. "Sometimes the only real negotiating tool is money. And if Gene can't give them anymore…" He stopped. The Clemmons kids were basically good people, but they were rough. Exactly the kind of rough Ashley had been sheltered from most of her life and dealing with them would provide the type of real life situation that might force her to realize she would much rather live with her dad in paradise than spend her days dickering with farmers. "Toby, what do you have planned for today?"

"Same as always."

Rick rose from his desk. "Think you can find me somebody to replace Ashley on mucking this morning?"

"You're setting her free?"

"I think today's the day she's going to set herself free."

He left the barn and strode to the main house. There was a light on in the kitchen, so he bounced up the steps to her porch and knocked on the back door.

Dressed in a clean T-shirt and jeans, Ashley answered the door. "I'm not late."

She walked to the butcher block in the center of the room and picked up her brick-red-colored mug.

Rick entered the enormous kitchen of the main house. Painted the same color as her mug, with oak cabinets everywhere, copper pots as decorations, and hardwood floors with southwest print rugs, the room looked more like something in the showroom of a building supply store than somebody's real kitchen.

"No, but you're also not mucking stalls today. Your dad's been negotiating with the Clemmons kids for their father's farm. We haven't heard from them in a few weeks. I thought today would be a good day to send somebody over and take their temperature. You up for it?"

She looked so surprised Rick almost felt bad for setting her up. But he had to. Managing a farm wasn't easy and he didn't think she had the finesse for it. Getting her to see that quickly was a kindness.

"Yes, I'm up for it."

"Great."

Chapter Four

Her dad would have worn khakis and a polo shirt. Ashley chose to wear a burnt-orange pantsuit for this meeting. She wasn't quite as casual as her dad, and she ultimately intended to put a more professional face on the name Seven Hills. The farm had always been stately and grand, but she had a vision of Seven Hills—known for nearly a dozen Kentucky Derby winners one of which just missed the triple crown—as being elegant.

She had even decided the night before that when she took control of the business, the staff would wear polo shirts with the farm's logo above the left breast, and uniform pants would replace jeans. She had also determined that she would keep the office in the main barn, and use the den and living room of the farmhouse for more important visitors like buyers.

Driving up Crescent Hill, then down the dirt lane of

the Clemmons farm, Ashley was very glad she owned an SUV. The closer she got to the house, the more rutted the road became and the more surrounded by trees. That was when she questioned her choice of heels.

Still, she exited her vehicle, putting her sunglasses in her brown leather briefcase since the multicolored canopy created by the fall leaves blocked the glare of the sun. She walked gingerly up the stone sidewalk to the simple white-frame house and knocked twice. A young woman opened the front door but not the screen door.

An odd sensation of warning rippled through her. The last screen door that hadn't opened to her had belonged to an angry Rick Capriotti.

"Can I help you?"

Ashley smiled. "I'm Ashley Meljac."

"I know who you are."

"Great, then you probably know my dad's been talking with your brothers about buying your farm."

The young woman turned and yelled, "Jake! That Meljac girl is here to see you."

Ashley took a breath. Nerves danced along her skin. The screen door hadn't opened yet, but she was getting an audience with the oldest Clemmons son. She couldn't believe Rick had so easily handed her her big chance to prove herself, but he had. And she began to wonder if he hadn't finally realized she didn't intend to give up, so he was bucking for the job of assistant manager. Which wouldn't be such a bad idea. With her at the helm and Rick as backup, as well as available for advice, they would be an unbeatable team.

Jake Clemmons appeared at the front door. He didn't open the screen, either. Still, Ashley didn't panic. Her father had only completed the beginning phases of negotiation. The screen door might not open until they were a little further along.

"What do you want?"

Ashley smiled. "You're negotiating with my dad to sell your farm. I'm just here to see how your decision is coming on that."

Jake opened the screen door and Ashley's heart flip-flopped. He was going to let her in!

She shifted her briefcase to step inside the house, but was blocked when Jake leaned forward and spit a stream of tobacco that cleared the porch and landed in the front yard.

"You here to offer us more money?"

Not wanting to insult the man with a shiver of disgust, Ashley held it back, settling for a quiet breath before she calmly said, "I've seen my dad's last offer and it was generous."

"There are six of us who live here. Six of us who will need new places to live if we sell this house and six of us who want to use that money as a jump-start. Your dad's going to have to come up with a better offer than what we got."

"So you aren't accepting my dad's offer?"

Jake laughed. "Ain't that what I just said?" He spit again, narrowly missing her jacket sleeve.

"Yes. That's exactly what you said. I just wanted to be clear."

"So you offering us more money?"

"No." She wasn't authorized to offer more money, and she suddenly saw what Rick had done. He hadn't handed her a big chance. He'd sent her here thinking he would scare her. Or to show her she was out of her element. But either way she looked like a jackass. Particularly to the Clemmonses who were expecting a raised bid.

"You know what? I'm going to go back and talk to my manager, Rick Capriotti, and see if the budget will allow us to raise our offer."

Jake smiled. "That's right neighborly of you."

Ashley said, "You're welcome," turned and walked to her SUV. She wasn't unnerved by the Clemmonses. She wasn't upset by tobacco chewing. She didn't care if the men cursed around her, or if she had to muck stalls, and do legitimate errands that sent her into town looking like a refugee from a manure factory. She did, however, hate being made to look like an idiot.

She left the Clemmons farm, drove to Seven Hills's main barn, jumped out of her SUV, strode into Rick's office and slammed the door. "Today is the day you can consider yourself fired."

He glanced up. "You can't fire me."

"No, but when I tell my dad you sent me to the Clemmonses to scare me, I'm sure he'll fire you."

"Why? For upsetting his precious daughter?" He leaned back in his chair so far the two front wheels came off the ground. The position showed off his lean frame and long legs and drew her attention to the point that she nearly lost her train of thought.

Ashley shook her head, annoyed with herself for noticing. "No, but he will fire you for putting us in a position where we now have to raise our bid on the Clemmons farm."

Rick's chair fell to the floor with a thump. "I didn't authorize you to raise our bid!"

"Well, I did it anyway because you might be able to manipulate me, but I wasn't going to let you manipulate the Clemmonses. They're nice people. They need money. The farm is their only bargaining chip for a jump-start on life. When I went there today they were expecting a raised offer. I refused to disappoint them."

"That's not how negotiating works. You have to start thinking carrot and stick. Give them something to reach for while subtly warning them that if they don't reach they'll lose."

"And that's not how I work. I am fair, Mr. Capriotti. I do not trick people."

With that she marched out of the office and to the farmhouse. Striding toward the den, she shucked her suit jacket and dropped it onto one of the upholstered chairs around the shiny cherrywood table of the huge formal dining room. She yanked the scarf from around her neck and tossed it onto an antique French provincial table in the long hall. Without breaking stride, she flung off her high heels, letting them land with a thump by the waterfall built into the wall across from the stained-glass front door.

By the time she reached the den, she wore only her suit trousers and the little white tank top she had beneath the jacket. She strode to the desk, snatched up the receiver of the phone and dialed the number for her dad's cell phone.

"Hello."

"Daddy, it's me."

"Hey, Ash, how's it going? You learning a lot?"

"Yeah," she said, sinking to the chair behind the desk. It was so good to hear her dad's relaxed, confident voice that she settled down, too. "I'm learning a lot more than I thought I would."

"Rick's a great guy. Smart guy. You wouldn't have believed his résumé. He bummed around on the rodeo circuit, then just stopped and finished his degree. Got a job on Tuscarora," he said, naming one of the biggest horse farms in Tennessee, "then like a gift from God he came back to me."

"Yeah, well, your gift of God just sent me to the Clemmonses' farm."

"Really?"

"He wanted me to take their temperature on the sale."

"And?"

"And they were expecting a raised offer."

To Ashley's surprise, her dad laughed. "Those cagey dogs."

"Those cagey dogs need money."

Her dad laughed again. "You fell for that?"

Ashley sat up in her chair.

"Ash, they're filthy rich. Their daddy socked away every cent he ever earned. They could all live in the south of France if they wanted. They choose to live here. They play hillbilly because they think it keeps people from taking advantage of them. But they aren't dumb."

Once again feeling like an idiot, Ashley rose from her seat to pace behind the desk in front of the wall of windows. Beyond the rich green grass of the backyard and past the main access road that separated the house grounds from the actual farm grounds, Rick stood by the section of fence that she knew was in line for repair, gesturing to one of the hands.

"So Rick gave you a little baptism by fire?"

"Or something," Ashley said, not quite sure what Rick was up to, but realizing that if she got him fired it would be a hollow victory. His tricks continually made her look like a fool, but that was exactly why she longed to beat him fair and square. To prove herself. If she was going to win this little contest they were in—and she would—she wanted it to be because she had shown herself to be the smarter of the two of them.

"And you came out of your Clemmonses' visit okay?"

"Yeah, I'm fine."

"You didn't call me to insist I fire Rick."

Staring through the big window at the man in question, Ashley managed a laugh. "No," she said, letting go of her big chance to get Rick fired, but determined to beat Rick. Really beat him. Show him she was so damned good they wouldn't even need him as second in command.

"Then why did you call?"

She swallowed. "I just missed you."

"Well, I'm having a ball here," her dad was saying when Rick began unbuttoning his shirt. Ashley tried to force her attention back to what her dad was saying, but when Rick shrugged out of his shirt, she forgot all about her dad and leaned forward to get a closer look. What was he doing?

"I can't wait to take you sailing, Ash. There's nothing like it. Hot sun, salt breezes. The freedom. I can't explain it."

"It sounds great," Ashley said, mesmerized by the sight at the fence. Bare chest glistening in the sun, Rick centered a post in a predug hole and lifted a mallet, as if demonstrating the installation procedure to the worker. Then he swung and hit the wooden column with the mallet, sending all his muscles into rippling motion.

She swallowed. Wow. Watching him was like seeing poetry in motion. He was that toned and fit…and gorgeous.

"Maybe you could think about coming to the islands for the holidays."

Mad at herself for not paying attention to her dad, Ashley put her mind back on the phone call. "I'm sorry. What did you say?"

"I'd like you to think about coming down for the holidays."

Surprised by that, Ashley turned away from the window. "I'd love to come down for the holidays," she said, but she couldn't prevent herself from turning to gaze out the window at Rick again.

She squeezed her eyes shut. What the hell was she doing? After two weeks of wishing she could spend the holiday with her dad, losing focus in her first real conversation with him didn't make any sense.

"This afternoon, I'll call my travel agent for arrangements for the Thanksgiving trip."

"Why not just come down for Thanksgiving and go home after New Year's Day?"

"Because I'm trying to learn how to run the farm, re-member?"

"Oh right," her dad replied. "I forgot."

Ashley sunk to the seat of the desk again. Now *that* didn't make any sense. Her dad was too smart to forget something as important as his daughter training to take over his beloved farm. Suddenly his offer of a visit to the islands didn't seem as wonderful as it had two seconds before. It seemed contrived. As if somebody had put him up to it. Maybe to get her away from the farm?

There was only one person who might have done it. Rick. He could have even called while she was walking up to the house, warned her dad that she was about to call him, and told her dad to get her out of his hair.

Flooded with disappointment, Ashley said, "I'm doing fine, Daddy. In fact, I'm doing great."

And if Rick Capriotti had told him otherwise, she'd just made *him* look foolish. By the time her father returned in February, she would know how to run every facet of this farm. And Rick would be so far away she hoped she'd never hear his name again.

When Ashley didn't return to the barn after lunch, Rick was confused. From the way she'd blown out of the office, he knew she intended to call her dad imme-diately and he'd expected her to come skipping down the path to the main barn and make a show out of kicking him out. Yet a full hour had gone by since she stormed away and he hadn't seen hide nor hair of her.

Of course, her dad might have said he wanted to fire

Rick personally since he was Seven Hills's owner. Gene wouldn't disrespect Rick by firing him through a second party. He had liked Rick and his credentials too much for that.

Rick frowned. Gene *had* liked him. He had been very impressed with Rick's experience and education and was thrilled to have him running Seven Hills.

Rick's frown deepened. No. Gene's reaction was more than plain happiness. When Rick really thought about it, he realized Ashley's dad had been relieved to find somebody so capable on such short notice. Gene had behaved like a man who could finally retire because he'd found the person into whose care he could entrust his beloved farm.

Which meant there was a third possibility to Rick's drama with Gene's daughter. Ashley might have whined to her dad that she wanted Rick fired, but Gene could very well have refused her.

Rick grinned. That scenario made the most sense. Gene wasn't as wrapped around his little girl's finger as half the people in Calhoun Corners believed and even though he planned to retire he still loved his farm. He wouldn't leave it in the hands of an amateur. He might have even told Ashley to stop playing farmhand and get involved with something that suited her.

Now *that* sounded like something Gene Meljac would say.

Shoving himself out of the old wooden office chair, Rick grinned again. This situation was simply too rich with possibility to ignore.

He strode out of the barn and up to the house and

knocked on the kitchen door, but no one answered. Hoping Ashley was still talking to "Daddy," he reached for the doorknob and let himself in.

Stepping into the kitchen he heard the sounds of singing. Off-key and a cappella, it couldn't have been a song on a radio or from a CD player so Rick turned to the right, toward the sound, wondering if Ashley had her own office. But when he stepped into the open doorway of the room where the singing was coming from he didn't see a desk and chair. He saw a washer and dryer and Ashley shimming a pair of worn jeans over skimpy red lace panties.

He tried to step back or choke out a warning that he was behind her so she didn't turn, but his throat had tightened shut. The image of those red lace panties combined with the sight of the thin red straps of her bra against the satiny white skin of her back had literally stolen his breath. She grabbed a T-shirt from the dryer, slid it over her head and turned.

When she saw him her mouth fell open, but she didn't speak.

Miraculously Rick found his voice. "From the jeans and T-shirt you're wearing, I'm guessing you're going back to work, which means Daddy wouldn't fire me."

She pushed past him, brushing her arm and thigh against his as she strode into the kitchen. "I didn't ask him to."

His heart pounding, Rick forced a laugh through his still-tight throat. "Right."

She spun to face him. "I didn't. You know why? Because when I was talking to him on the phone I realized this isn't about Daddy. It's about you and me. Who's better. I have the advantage of actually owning the farm."

He'd seen lots of scantily dressed women in his lifetime. Hell, he'd seen lots of women naked. *Lots.* And Ashley hadn't even been naked; he'd only gotten a glimpse of her back. But it wasn't her physical body that had enticed him and made him curious. It was her choice of red lacy panties and bra beneath scruffy jeans and a ratty T-shirt. It reminded him that she slept in a virtually see-through pink nightie and it caused him to realize that Ashley didn't just like pretty things; she used them to express her personality. Soft pink for bed. Red lace when she expected to have to fight him.

He didn't know whether to be frightened or flattered.

"Your dad owns the farm."

"But I will someday, so it's a given that he'll make me the manager if he feels I can do the job. That's my edge. You, on the other hand, actually have the knowledge and experience I need. That's your edge."

"And it's a damn good one."

"I never said it wasn't. But the way I see this, all I have to do is survive."

But that wasn't what she intended. The red lace panties said she planned to fight.

"What are you grinning at?"

He shook his head. "You."

She marched over and stood in front of him, in his space as he'd done to her when he wanted to intimidate her. He had to admit she was a quick learner and more of a challenge than he would have guessed.

"You don't think I'm ready for a fight?"

"Oh, honey, I know you're ready for a fight. I saw the red panties and bra. That's underwear that gives a woman courage."

Her chin lifted. "How would you know that?"

"You gonna deny it?"

She took a soft breath, as if to say she refused to be baited but he smiled. Ran his finger along her soft chin. Bent his head and kissed her.

He had intended to give her a light peck on the lips, but her mouth was soft and inviting. Rick tumbled into a full-blown kiss as naturally and easily as breathing. The warmth of pleasure mixed and mingled with tingles of arousal, and urged him to take, to satisfy, to explore, to mate. His brain stumbled over that word, but his instincts didn't. In a very short time, probably because of the intensity of their fight and the intensity of their attraction, they'd gotten to the heart of each other's personality and he knew he could sleep with her. Not just sexually, but romantically. But that was worse. Lust was one thing. It was simple and manageable. Romance was another. The last time he'd romanced a woman she broke his heart, left him to raise the baby alone and sent him into hiding.

He jerked away, his shivers of pleasure and arousal now shivers of fear.

Rubbing his hand along the back of his neck, trying to short-circuit the wave of emotions pouring through him, he said, "Okay, that was an accident."

Ashley only stared at him, her breath coming in short, quick gasps, her green eyes dazed.

"I'm sorry."

A spark of anger quickly replaced the dazed look in her eyes. He didn't blame her. He could kick himself for kissing her. It was just plain stupid. And might be the one thing she could tell her dad that really would get him fired.

But she didn't threaten to get him fired. She grabbed her jacket from the back of a kitchen chair and headed for the door. "Let's just get the hell back to the barn."

Tossing manure with more force than was necessary, Ashley tried to forget about that kiss. But it was no use. With a quick press of his mouth and a few practiced moves, that idiot had weakened her knees and sent her blood singing through her veins in the most extraordinary way. She might have thought he'd done it to remind her that unless she wanted to get her father involved, he was still the boss, except that he'd said the kiss was an accident.

Accident?

How did one accidentally kiss somebody? She hadn't noticed anybody bumping into his back forcing him forward and their lips into intimate contact.

Rick entered the barn and began striding toward the office and Ashley snorted with disgust. Accident her foot! That kiss was no damned accident.

So why had he said that? Better yet, why *had* he kissed her? She stopped shoveling, angled the shovel scoop into the floor and leaned on the handle. Why *had* he kissed her?

Knowing that if she didn't get back to work, she wouldn't get to her house before eight that night, Ashley put her shovel in motion again, but she didn't stop thinking about the kiss. Or the feelings. Dear Lord, she didn't want to revive her rubbery knees and tingling toes. So she thought about the direction of the discussion right before the kiss. She remembered that he'd seen her standing in her red underwear, wiggling into her jeans and pulling on a clean T-shirt and it all became abundantly clear. *He* was attracted to *her.*

She laughed and two horses whinnied. Well now. This was certainly a horse of a different color. And maybe a way to put them on even footing again. This might even be her real bargaining chip to get him to show her the things she really needed to learn to run the farm.

Now all she had to do was figure out the best time and the best way to "use" this attraction card she'd drawn. Whatever she chose to do, she had to make this count.

Chapter Five

Driving up the guesthouse access road, Rick snapped his cell phone closed, then suppressed a strong urge to curse. He wasn't upset that Tia was sick, he was upset that life wouldn't stop throwing him curves. Today he was in parent hell, needing, as parents so frequently do, to be in two places at once. He had to decide between going to work to do payroll, the one job on the farm that only he could oversee, and taking care of a baby that only his family knew about.

He frowned. Technically his family weren't the only people who knew about Ruthie. He swerved to the right and picked up the main road to the Seven Hills residence. Ashley knew about Ruthie, too.

Rick jerked his truck to a stop in front of Ashley's kitchen door, reminding himself that the way to handle this was to negotiate. Not beg. Not give away all his advantage. But standing on her back porch, holding Ruthie huddled against him, Rick knew he was probably going to lose his advantage. If he were in Ashley's position, he most certainly wouldn't do a favor for his competition and if he did, he would make her pay. If Ashley were smart, his asking her to babysit would be the straw that broke the camel's back of their little game. Nonetheless, because payroll was the one job that couldn't be put off, and because he'd promised Gene he'd run his farm without a hitch, Rick knocked twice.

The kitchen light was on. Still, despite the cold morning air, he had learned his lesson about walking in on Ashley and he waited on the porch, checking to be sure Ruthie's blanket was securely around her.

A few seconds later, Ashley opened the kitchen door. "Have another important mission for me?" she asked, not looking at him, as she swept away from the door, her long red nightgown billowing around her.

Forgetting all about his reasons for being at her door, Rick only stared. Her nightgown and cover-up weren't revealing. They were simply pretty. Feminine. And she looked right at home in them.

"I know I'm late," she said, her back to him as she poured herself a cup of coffee. "But I didn't think you'd mind."

Over the bunch of Ruthie's blanket, he glanced at his watch, and his eyes narrowed. She *was* late and from the casual tone of her voice she didn't care. She might have even been expecting him to come after her. And if she expected him to come after her, her being in the pretty red satin getup was deliberate.

"Want some coffee?" Ashley asked as she turned to face him, but as if only now noticing Ruthie, her facial expression and tone of voice went from carefree to concerned. "Oh my goodness! What's wrong?"

"Nothing. Well, Ruthie's not sick or anything. She's fine."

Ashley visibly relaxed.

"But Tia is sick."

"Your sister?"

"She normally watches Ruthie, but she has a virus. My mom doesn't want to risk Ruthie catching it and I agree. But that leaves me without a sitter." Their gazes met across the kitchen. "I have to do payroll today and you're the only other person who knows about Ruthie."

Ashley set her coffee on the counter and said, "Okay, give me two minutes to get dressed and we'll go."

"Go?"

"To your house. I'm sure you don't want me to watch her here."

"It's probably not a good idea."

"So I'll change and you can drive us all to the guesthouse."

He nodded and she left the room, pretty red bedclothes billowing around her. Ruthie stirred on his shoulder, but Rick rocked her back to sleep and then called his mother to let her know Ashley would be looking after Ruthie. Pacing the kitchen for the next few minutes, he glanced at copper pots hanging above the center island, studied the reddish colored countertops, walked over southwest print rugs, noticing that the room was unexpectedly homey. Gene wasn't exactly a homey guy. He liked to impress people. And though the kitchen was impressive, the warmth of it surprised Rick until he realized Ashley had probably decorated this home.

"Okay, I'm ready."

"Good." Rick said, turning to face Ashley who smiled at him. She should have used his need of a babysitter to her advantage, but she hadn't. Instead she behaved as if this were a simple favor for a friend. Indescribable relief flooded him.

"I really appreciate this."

Shrugging into a denim jacket, she said, "Yeah, well, once again, remember I'm keeping this secret for Ruthie's sake, not for yours. You and I are still competitors."

Her reminder that they were rivals caused Rick to stop halfway to her door. They *were* rivals, and she had been expecting him to come to her kitchen to reprimand her about being late, yet she was wearing a billowy red nightgown. Which meant her outfit had been her next move in their competition.

Rick laughed. "Now I get it." He opened the door, stepped out onto the porch and started down the steps to his truck with Ashley behind him. "That was what the nightgown was all about. You were running some kind of game to try to trip me up in our competition."

"I wasn't running some kind of game," Ashley said, rounding the truck as Rick tucked Ruthie into her car seat. "I was running late."

"Right. That's why you were still in your nightgown. A pretty red one. Not the nearly see-through thing you had on a few days ago. A nice covering nightgown so that it wouldn't look obvious you were trying to…to…"

"To what, smarty-pants?"

He jumped behind the steering wheel. "I don't know." He grinned across the seat at her. "Maybe make me weak with lust?"

She laughed.

"I know I'm right."

"Which makes me right and accomplishes what I wanted to accomplish."

Rick steered the truck to the guesthouse access road. "I don't have a clue what you're talking about."

"I'm talking about the fact that you're as attracted to me as I am to you."

"Hardly."

"Oh, Rick, Rick, Rick. It is impossible to kiss somebody accidentally. It's too hard to get two mouths together for it to happen as a matter of chance."

Confused, he glanced over at her. "What?"

"You said yesterday that our kiss was an accident. But think it through. There is no way a kiss can happen accidentally."

He drew a long breath.

"That can only mean that the "accidental" part of that kiss had to be that you "accidentally" slipped up and let your attraction to me get the better of you."

Pulling his truck into the parking space beside the guesthouse, he said nothing. He sure as hell wasn't going to tell her she was right.

She laughed. "You are so easy to read. Every time I'm right about something you simply don't talk."

"You want me to talk. All right, I'll talk." He pushed open the truck door, jumped out, slammed his door closed, then opened the extended cab door to get Ruthie. "Prancing around in your underwear in front of me is a schoolgirl's game. If you really want to run this farm you have to stop thinking like a girl and start thinking like a businessperson."

"And that's the other thing you do when I have you over a barrel. If being quiet doesn't work to keep you from having to discuss something, you change the subject."

She just wasn't going to let that kiss go. He sighed. "Okay. Fine. The reason that kiss was an accident is because nothing good can come of our attraction." He stopped fiddling with the straps of the car seat and caught Ashley's gaze. "That's right. *Our* attraction. You and I are attracted to each other. But we're also competing for the same job."

He took Ruthie from her car seat and jogged up the steps to the porch.

Ashley jumped out of the truck and was right behind him. "So what you're really saying is that we shouldn't use the attraction to get the better of each other in our competition."

He sighed with relief. "Yes."

"You would have used it."

He stepped into the foyer and immediately started up the steps. She was right again. If he hadn't been as attracted to her as she was to him, he would have used it. But with both of them attracted, neither one of them had the advantage.

"But I'm not." He paused on the steps and glanced down at her. "By the way, I'm putting Ruthie in her crib. She may sleep another hour or so."

Ashley nodded. "Okay. But I still say you would have used the attraction."

He walked into the nursery, laid Ruthie in the crib, kissed her forehead and was running down the steps again within seconds. "I can't and neither can you. Since our attraction is mutual, neither one of us has an advantage. But even beyond that there's something else you need to think about."

Obviously not believing him, she crossed her arms on her chest.

Rick shook his head. "There's something more important you need to consider in this little attraction of ours and that's how it's going to play in town."

She frowned. "Our being attracted?"

"Do you really want everybody gossiping that you're prancing around in front of me in your underwear?"

"Two of the three times you saw me in 'underwear' I was actually wearing a nightgown. The other time, *you* walked in on me."

"But today I didn't. Today you were prancing and I have a feeling you hadn't intended to stop there. Once you had me rattled you were going to continue teasing me in front of Toby and anybody else who got within hearing distance. To embarrass me and to keep me rattled. But your game would have backfired." Recognizing from the expression on her face that she wasn't getting what he was telling her, he combed his fingers through his hair. "Everybody in this town thinks I'm an opportunist, con artist."

"Which gives me an advantage."

"Which makes you look like an idiot who didn't

learn her lesson from the opportunist she married if you as much as flirt with me. That's why the attraction has to come off the bargaining table as much as Ruthie had to come off."

She frowned and studied his face for a few seconds. "You're taking our attraction out of play for *my* benefit?"

He rolled his eyes and headed for the door. "I'm doing this for me, too. Do you think it's fun to be called an opportunist?"

Her frown deepened. "Wow. I never thought of it that way. I guess that when my husband was taking ten million dollars of my trust fund I never realized how much it would hurt him to be called an opportunist."

"Exactly my point. *I* don't want your money. I'm not an opportunist. And you really don't want anything to do with the likes of me. So, neither one of us needs the gossip." He caught the doorknob. "Thanks for watching Ruthie."

She took a breath. "I'm not sure I know what I'm doing."

"My mother's only a phone call away. She would have kept Ruthie, but my dad pops in and out of the house all day, and she didn't want him to discover her." He caught her gaze. "She said that even if you don't call she'll stop by around ten or so to check on things."

Ashley nodded.

"I'll be back for lunch."

In only a few minutes of caring for Ruthie, Ashley realized it did not take a genius to figure out how to perform the basics for a baby. First, there were bottles in the refrigerator. Second, there were directions on the box of rice cereal. Third, all one had to do was test out a baby's strength and level of body control to know how to keep a good hold on her in the little baby bathtub. By the time Rick's mother arrived, Ashley and Ruthie had bonded and were watching reruns of soap operas on a satellite channel.

"Oh, she loves the soaps!" Elizabeth Capriotti crooned, setting a red and white cooler on the floor so she could take Ruthie from Ashley's arms. A medium height woman with brown hair and soft green eyes, Elizabeth looked too young to be the mother of the guy currently competing with Ashley.

"I wonder if she got her love of soaps from her mom?"

Elizabeth cringed. "Who knows what she got from her mom. I'm hoping the people who claim nurture beats out nature are correct," she said, settling Ruthie on her left arm so she could take her cooler to the kitchen and set it on the table. "I brought lunch."

"You didn't have to!"

"I know, but Rick feels guilty about asking you to watch Ruthie. I figured if you could tell him I brought lunch it might alleviate some of his guilt."

Ashley laughed. "You're a good mom."

Frowning, Elizabeth turned from the table. "I don't think anyone's ever told me that."

"That's because most of us take our mothers for granted." Ashley had been a model child, always working to please her parents. Yet, after her mother's death, she remembered a hundred times her mother had done things for her that she hadn't properly acknowledged. She had long ago forgiven herself, but that didn't mean it didn't hurt to sometimes recall the times and ways she'd taken her mother for granted.

Elizabeth's eyes softened. "I'm sorry. I forgot you lost your mom."

"That was years ago," Ashley said, brushing aside Rick's mother's concern because she didn't want people to feel sorry for her. "But the sentiment is still true. Everybody takes his or her mother for granted."

"I guess," Elizabeth said, handing the baby back to Ashley so she could open the cooler to pull out the sandwiches and drinks. "But in the end, it all balances out. There's a great deal of satisfaction in mothering."

Ruthie cooed and Ashley shifted her on her arm. "Yeah. I've been watching Ruthie about three hours and already I understand that."

"You look good with a baby. You're going to make a good mother yourself."

Ashley laughed. "That will be the day."

Elizabeth turned from the table. "You don't want to have children?"

"I don't want to have a husband."

Elizabeth looked aghast. "You don't?"

"I see you've forgotten my other life trauma. My huge mistake of a marriage." She cringed. "A girl doesn't lose half her trust fund without getting skeptical of men."

"I hear you," Elizabeth agreed and turned back to the table. She pulled a pie from the bottom of the cooler, lifted the lid off the plastic container and sent the mouth-watering aroma of freshly baked apples and cinnamon into the air. "I baked this this morning."

Ashley groaned in ecstasy. "That smells heavenly."

"It's Rick's favorite."

"As I said, you're a good mom."

Busy fussing over the pie, Elizabeth said, "Right about now Rick needs some good mothering."

Ashley glanced at Ruthie. "It couldn't have been easy to have a baby dumped on his doorstep."

"If that had been how it happened, Rick might have been okay. But it wasn't. Jen showed up at his apartment with the baby and made it seem she was back."

"Back?"

"Back in Rick's life." Elizabeth sighed. "Rick adored her. I'm not a hundred percent sure why. From the stories he tells she made him miserable." Elizabeth went back to arranging the food on the table. "Anyway, she arrived at his door one night, with the baby, and told him leaving had been a mistake and she wanted them to be a family. He was ecstatic. So, when he woke up alone with the baby, and then found the note that all but threatened legal action if he tried to come after her or money for Ruthie, the blow was devastating."

"Because he hated her accusing him of wanting her money?"

Elizabeth shook her head sadly. "No, because he loved her. God knows why." Finished with arranging lunch, she reached for Ruthie again. "He did a lot of growing up when Jen left him the first time. He realized he couldn't bum around on the rodeo circuit forever and finished the degree he had started before he lost patience and more or less ran away."

Ashley laughed. "He ran away from college?"

Elizabeth shrugged. "He was bored. And immature. So he bailed out. But when Jen left him with the baby, he didn't run. The decisions he made this time were correct."

"You mean coming home?"

Elizabeth nodded, then kissed Ruthie. "To family."

Ashley smiled, but inside her heart melted. This was the difference between mothers and fathers. Elizabeth wanted her son to come home. He was in trouble, so she wanted to circle the wagons around Rick to help him. Conversely Ashley's dad was tossing her out of his life, backhandedly telling her to get her own life. Forget about family. Forge an identity—and not necessarily at the farm—then visit.

"Anyway, he bounced back the first time Jen hurt him. He'll bounce back this time, too."

Ashley smiled and nodded, but she understood what Elizabeth was saying. He would rebound more quickly this time because his family would help him.

"That's why his father and I were so grateful when your dad gave him this job. Ben doesn't know about Ruthie," Elizabeth said, referring to her husband. "We're more or less keeping her from him. Because of his heart attack last year we don't want him overstressed. He just thinks Jen came back into Rick's life then dumped him again. He knows Rick took a real blow to his self-esteem." She paused to laugh. "But Ben's no dummy. He's easily figured out that Rick finished his degree hoping Jen would come back and that Rick spent the year she was gone working toward "deserving" her. When she left him the second time it was like saying that no matter what Rick did he wasn't good enough. So even if this job is only for three months while your dad's away, Rick needed the stamp of approval your dad gave him. Not only saying that he was good enough to run his farm, but also that he's good enough to train his daughter." She smiled at Ashley. "It means a lot."

Ashley nodded, a small wave of guilt rippling through her for wanting the job that was so perfect for Rick. But she refused to fall victim to it. As far as she was concerned, Rick had many more advantages than she did. He had family, people who cared about him, and experience. He could get a job with a snap of his fingers. Ashley had to prove herself at Seven Hills. No one else would give her this kind of chance.

"The job means a lot to me, too."

"And that's why Rick's going to see to it that you're trained right," Elizabeth said, smiling at Ashley as if she didn't know Ashley and Rick were competing for the job. Which confused Ashley. It didn't make sense for him not to tell his parents that he had a very good shot of getting this job permanently and a good shot at staying in Calhoun Corners permanently. It almost appeared as if he were preparing them for his leaving.

"Anyway, I have to get back home to whip up lunch for Ben so he doesn't ask what I've been doing all morning." She planted a noisy kiss on Ruthie's temple, causing Ruthie to giggle and slap her with a rattle. "I'll see you later, sweetie."

She handed Ruthie to Ashley again, waved goodbye at the front door and left.

Ashley was still thinking about the conversation that night as she drove to the diner for dinner. She didn't want to get too optimistic and think deep down that Rick believed she was going to win their competition, but that was what it seemed. Why else would he let his family believe this job was only temporary, and not tell them he and Ashley were competing.

Pushing open the glass diner door she said hello to Ellen who looked up from the cash register. "Hey, what's up, sugar?"

"I had an easy day today." Having cared for Ruthie for the past fourteen hours, Ashley wasn't a filthy, smelly mess when Rick returned from his day's duties. So instead of heating a frozen entrée, she had decided to treat herself to supper in town. "And I thought I'd celebrate by having dinner with you."

"Then let me set you up at the counter so we can talk."

"Great." Ashley slid onto a stool as Ellen put a place mat and silverware in front of her. "What will it be?"

"I see beef stew is today's special," Ashley said nodding at the chalkboard beside the door to the kitchen. "That sounds good."

"One bowl of stew coming up."

The bell above the door rang and as Ellen shifted to put in Ashley's order, Ashley turned to see who was at the door. Rayne Fegan entered.

Wearing loose jeans and a sleeveless cotton blouse and with the bangs of her blond hair falling over the thick lenses of her big-framed glasses, Rayne wasn't exactly attractive. But Ashley didn't think she wanted to be. She had been one of the geeky girls a few grades below Ashley in high school, and Ashley remembered that she liked being the supersmart daughter of the editor of the *Chronicle*. Even in high school Rayne knew she had the power of the press behind her.

When she saw Ashley her eyes lit up and she headed for the stool beside Ashley's.

"Mind if I sit here?"

Ashley knew why she felt uncomfortable having Rayne sit beside her. Her dad, the editor of the *Calhoun Corners Chronicle* supported Mayor Capriotti's competition. His biggest contribution to Auggie Malloy's effort was making the mayor look bad in editorials and Rayne was the one digging up dirt for her dad to print.

And Ashley knew Rick's secret. Worse, it had already almost slipped out once at Janie Alberter's dress shop.

Nonetheless, not wanting to alert Rayne that Ashley might know something worth printing, Ashley said, "Please, have a seat."

"What's new at the farm?" Rayne asked, sliding onto the stool and grabbing a menu from the holder beside the salt and pepper shakers.

"Not much."

"I heard your dad hired Rick Capriotti."

"Only temporarily. My dad's taking sailing lessons in the Bahamas. When he comes home, Rick moves on."

Rayne laughed. "Right."

Ashley glanced at her, not sure if she was trying to egg Ashley into saying something to defend Rick or if Rayne merely wasn't a fan of the Capriotti family as a whole since her father clearly wasn't. Sticking to the facts to keep herself out of trouble, Ashley said, "He's actually training me to take over."

Rayne laughed again. "And you believed that. Jeez,

Ash, we all thought you learned your lesson when you lost your trust fund."

The jab would have hit its mark, except Rick had warned her that any relationship between them would cause this kind of snide remark. Prepared for it, Ashley felt nothing. Not even a ripple of unease.

Ellen walked out of the kitchen, holding a steaming bowl of stew. "Here you go."

Rayne put the menu back in its holder. "That looks good. I'll have a bowl of stew, too."

Ellen nodded and walked away. Ashley picked up her fork and started eating.

"Rick's back for a reason," Rayne said. "I can feel it in my bones. From the fact that you're not talking much, I'm guessing that you believe just as I do that while he's pretending to train you, he's actually getting his foot in the door with your dad to take the job himself."

"And what if he is?" Ashley asked quietly. "Even if he and I are in a full-blown competition for this job, what difference does it make?"

"I talked with Bert. He told me the two of you were competing and that from the way you were behaving when you came to pick up a part it was clear you wanted the job. It makes me angry that Rick thinks he can stroll into town and run you off."

Ashley sighed. "He's not running me off. I have the edge of being heir to the farm. Even if he wins this round, and my dad makes him manager when he comes home in February, eventually I'll inherit Seven Hills and then there won't be any question of who's boss."

"Except your dad is what? Forty-five? Forty-six? He

could live another forty years. If you don't win this fight and your dad hires Rick, you'll watch him doing your job for forty long years. Is that what you want?"

Ashley struggled not to close her eyes in frustration. Not because Rayne was badgering her, but because everything Rayne said was true. Her dad was too young for Ashley to count on inheriting the farm. When her dad returned in February, if she wasn't prepared, Rick would get the job. And what would she do for forty years? Sit back and watch her competition living the life she wanted? Act as Rick's hostess on the farm? Have everybody believe Rick had pulled a fast one on her to steal her job away?

Still none of this was Rayne's concern and Ashley wasn't about to let Rayne bait her. "Regardless of what happens, it's none of your business."

"It is if you and I strike a deal."

Ashley looked at her. "Why would I strike a deal with you?"

"Because you want to run that farm and from what I hear Rick has you shoveling manure. He has absolutely no intention of giving up the manager job at Seven Hills. But if public opinion suddenly swung against him, such as, if you found out that he was fired from his last job or something, my dad could put it in an editorial, and just like the last time public opinion swung against him, Rick would run."

Ashley snorted a laugh. From her talk with Elizabeth that morning Ashley knew that "running" was the last thing Rick wanted to do. He had a family who longed to nurture him. If he left Calhoun Corners it would only be to find work. If he got the job at Seven Hills, he would stay forever. The only way he'd run would to be to protect Ruthie. But that was what Rayne was saying. Rick wouldn't leave the comfort of his family without a good reason and Ashley knew how to push him. All Ashley had to do would be drop one little hint about his secret—even something as small as Jen Martin's name—and Rick would be out of her hair.

Rayne caught her arm. "Ashley, something is going on with this guy. All my reporter's instincts are screaming. What if he's fleeing from an arrest or something? Do you really want him running your family's farm? You're the person in the position to find out what's going on and once you do, he'll leave and you'll be the one managing the farm."

Except she wouldn't have beaten Rick for the job. She would have tricked her way into it. She'd be no better than her ex-husband. And she was better. She was a hundred times better. She didn't cheat, lie, steal or make promises she didn't keep. She'd promised not to tell anyone about Ruthie and she wasn't going back on her word.

No matter what the cost.

"My dad doesn't hire anybody he doesn't first check out. I'm sure he investigated everything from Rick's credit rating to his potential arrest record. You're not going to find anything in Rick's past that my dad doesn't already know."

"Your dad might know everything about Rick, but mine doesn't and mine's the one with the power of the press."

"And mine's the one who counts." Ashley rose and

reached into her jeans pocket for a ten-dollar bill which she tossed on the counter.

"You're going to be sorry," Rayne called after Ashley as she left the diner.

Stepping out into the chilly end-of-October night, Ashley knew Rayne was right. She could get rid of Rick Capriotti just by telling his secret. Not that he had a child. But that his child had a well-known grandfather whose daughter did the very things her father preached against. One word to Rayne and Rick would find himself in the center of tabloid hell. Even if he got the job at Seven Hills, he wouldn't keep it.

But then Ruthie would become as much of an object of gossip as Rick. And Elizabeth would lose her bonding time with her granddaughter.

Cursing, Ashley jumped into her SUV. The sad truth was she couldn't fool herself anymore. She wasn't staying quiet for Elizabeth or Ben or even Ruthie. She was keeping this secret for Rick. He was taking her job, refused to have anything to do with her personally, and was driving her to distraction, and she was protecting him.

Not because she was a schmuck. But because it was the right thing to do. He was a nice guy who had been burned. Instead of screaming bloody murder over Jen Martin abandoning their daughter, or even trying to get some financial help from Jen's wealthy family, he'd quietly assumed his responsibility, like the mature, honest man that he was.

But nobody in town would ever believe that. Rick was right. They were both victims of their pasts.

Chapter Six

The next morning when Ashley walked into the barn, Rick tossed his pencil to the desk blotter, rose from his seat and met her in the aisle that divided the two long rows of stalls.

"You and I are going back up to your house."

Her eyes narrowed, as if she suspected this was some kind of trick, and he sighed. "Just follow me up to the house and hold the discussion until we get behind closed doors."

Though she stormed up to her back porch, she did as he requested. She didn't say a word until they were standing in the kitchen. But when he shut the door behind him and turned to face her, her arms were crossed on her chest and her expression was mutinous.

"Now what?"

"We're here because the computer in the den is the one that has all the financial information on it."

"So?"

"So we're starting a new phase of your training today."

The suspicion he saw in her eyes turned to cautious optimism. "And what phase is that?"

"Management." Knowing he owed her an explanation, he rubbed his hand along the back of his neck. "Last night I got to thinking about this deal. And I realized that you're right."

She gaped at him. "I'm *right?*"

"Yes. You're right. This is your farm. Your heritage. It would have been the perfect job for me had you not wanted it. But you do want it. And the second half of my assignment from your dad was to teach you how to do it." He drew a long breath. "So I'm going to teach you."

Her confused expression shifted into a look of pleasure. Her pretty green eyes warmed with joy. Her plump lips tipped into a smile.

He realized again how attractive she was but something new also struck him. His attraction to her wasn't totally about appearance. Sure, her looks were a big part of why he liked her. But she was also spontaneous. Or maybe pure. Not in a virginal sense, but in the sense that she either didn't or couldn't hold back her emotions. When she was angry, she yelled. When she was happy, she smiled.

"You're really going to teach me?"

"Yes."

"No secret manure pile back there?"

He laughed and something else amazing struck him.

Nobody made him laugh the way Ashley did. He couldn't even remember the last person who had tried to make him laugh, let alone somebody who made him laugh naturally.

"No secret manure pile. Yesterday when you babysat Ruthie, you proved that this isn't just a game to you. You take your responsibilities seriously. You do what needs to be done. You're not a spoiled pampered socialite… well, maybe a little, but when it comes to the farm you're serious. That means you deserve your shot. I don't have the right to take it from you. And I'm going to teach you."

"Wow."

There it was again. That wonderful spontaneity. He almost couldn't believe he hadn't noticed it before. But he was noticing today and reacting to it. He just plain liked being around her. But that was wrong. He'd already figured out he couldn't even be too friendly with her or the gossip would kill both of them.

"Yeah, well, let's see if you're still saying wow once I go over the three-tiered budget and the human resources things you need to know."

She took a breath. "I don't care how difficult this is. I'm excited."

He knew she was. He could see it on her face. And though it cost him to have to give up this job, he couldn't stop the pleasure that filled him. Teaching her was the right thing to do. But being pleased wasn't the right reaction to her excitement. With the sexual chemistry that raced between them, getting joy from her joy could inadvertently start them down a romantic path.

And that was wrong. Even if he didn't care about creating gossip, even if he wouldn't need to move on to find work when Gene came home, there was the matter of protecting Ruthie. If push came to shove in a custody battle with Senator Martin, Rick wouldn't hesitate to go into hiding. And he wouldn't be taking anybody with him. Especially not somebody who had so much to stay for the way Ashley did. In fact, she would be crazy to want to go on the run with him.

So, no. There would be no romance between him and Ashley.

Ashley and Rick worked in the den for about two hours. When the nuances of Seven Hills's accounting system had been explained, Rick needed to check something in the barn and left Ashley to familiarize herself with the financial state of the farm and the current budget. For two hours, she sat with her eyes glued to the computer screen, taking in not just where the money went, but the little things Rick hadn't told her to absorb. She noted the vendors and the names of the farms where they bought stallions or sold yearlings that weren't taken to auction, wondering why these vendors and farms were chosen and knowing she'd have to ask her dad.

After lunch Rick came back to the house. "I'm driving to the next county to look at a stallion."

"Okay."

She waited for him to tell her what to do while he was gone. Instead after an awkward pause he asked, "Do you want to drive or ride?"

"It doesn't matter," Ashley said, bouncing from the

seat behind her dad's big desk, realizing he didn't intend to ease into this transition and that meant that she had to be quicker to recognize his intentions.

"Then I'll drive." He turned and began walking out of the den. "And grab a jacket. It's cold."

Ashley raced upstairs, snatched a leather blazer from her closet to dress up her old jeans and met Rick at his truck, which was parked beside the barn. She tried not to let her pleasure show because she knew this wasn't easy for him. Technically he was training his boss, but more than that he had wanted this job. And he was the odds-on favorite in their head-to-head competition. Instead he was sacrificing the position that seemed tailor-made for him because he knew it was the right thing to do.

But he wasn't the only one who knew how to do the right thing, and she suddenly realized that he needed to know that when the chips were down, she could be a good guy, too.

"I ran into Rayne Fegan last night."

He took his eyes off the road long enough to cast a long look at her. "What did she want?"

"She wanted me to spy on you but I told her no."

He peered over at her again, this time, though, his lips quirked as if he were trying to keep himself from grinning. "She wanted you to spy and you told her no?"

"Even knowing you were my only stumbling block to running this farm, I refused to sell you out."

"Can I ask why?"

"Because it was the right thing to do. The same reason you're teaching me my job. We've both just proven that we're good people."

"Yeah, well your proof didn't cost you your job."

She shrugged. "I didn't know that at the time. At the time, I saw Rayne as presenting me with the opportunity to get rid of you, which would have made me a shoo-in for this job. Yet I decided that even if it meant losing the manager position to you I had to do the right thing and keep Ruthie a secret."

He took a breath. "I appreciate that."

"So we really are even."

"Finally."

"Yeah."

"Yeah."

The conversation died out and Ashley settled on the seat of his truck. For the first time in a long time she felt comfortable. Happy even.

The thought that she was happy surprised her so much that she peeked at Rick. She could easily admit she was "happy" to be learning the ropes of running the farm, but deep down inside she knew that was only part of it. Over the past few days she had won Rick's respect because she simply wouldn't give up but also because they were getting to know each other. Just that morning he'd said her babysitting Ruthie proved that she was determined and deserving. So in a way she'd won his respect the old-fashioned way. She'd earned it.

She'd *earned* it.

He hadn't bowed to her because she had money, because she would someday own the farm, or even because it had been an order of her dad. He'd conceded the job they both wanted because she'd proven herself.

Her eyes unexpectedly filled with tears. She'd never

realized that having somebody go against her could be good. But in this case it had. Not because she'd proven herself to Rick, but because she'd proven that she could fight. Losing to her ex-husband had stolen all the fight from her, all her courage, all her will. Rick refusing to budge had been the best thing anyone had ever done for her.

They arrived at the small horse farm and as they drove down the dirt lane, Ashley took in the pretty yellow house and barn surrounded by orange-leafed trees.

This was what she loved about her home. Everything in and around Calhoun Corners was clean, natural, real. Work was hard, but honest. Rewards were earned. And now she was part of it. Someday she might even be a big part.

When they reached the barn, Rick shut down the engine of the truck and turned to her. "Though you're the boss, you're still a manager in training. I talk in there."

She nodded. "Got it."

They both exited the vehicle and Rick waited for her to come around to his side, which was closer to the barn.

When she reached him he turned and began striding to the barn. "I'm guessing your dad forgot he put in a bid on this horse, because he never mentioned it to me. But this morning I got the call notifying us that ours was the winning bid."

Walking as fast as she could to keep up with Rick's long strides, Ashley debated telling Rick that her dad forgetting important things like bids was more proof that he was probably planning to retire and more proof that she wasn't learning to run Seven Hills a minute too soon. In the end she decided against it. In four short days they'd gone from enemies to friends. It wasn't that she didn't feel she'd known him long enough to trust him. It was more that he already knew more than she let most people know about her. Though the urge to talk to him and confide in him was natural, she knew how quickly and how easily people could take a simple confession of a doubt or even something unsettled in her life and use it against her.

So instead of confiding yet another fact of her life, she said, "What horse is this?"

"Sweet Potato."

Ashley laughed. "Sweet Potato?"

"Apparently that was the owner's pet name for his granddaughter."

"Thank goodness for reasonable explanations."

"Sweet Potato didn't win any big races. But he outperformed expectations. I'm guessing your dad thinks that his next generation will produce some big time winners."

"That would be my guess, too."

Rick cast a glance in her direction. "So you do know a little bit?"

"I know horses. You can't live around them all your life and not learn their quirks and intricacies."

"Running a horse farm is about more than horses."

"Okay. How about this then? I learned enough from living on the farm to recognize that even though we don't train or race, we're still in the gambling business. We scout races looking for horses like Sweet Potato, who can potentially produce a next generation of even faster horses. So we gamble on the stallions and mares we choose to breed, and we gamble on whether or not we can sell the foals produced."

Rick laughed. "It's a little more than that. But things like the accounting system, caring for the land and schmoozing at the races can be taught. If you don't know instinctively that business—any business—is about gambling, and that knowing even a sure thing is a risk or that the right choice is sometimes the one that looks like the wrong choice, you'll fail."

"I don't intend to fail."

"Gonna make lots of money, huh?"

"It isn't about money for me. It's about home. It's about keeping Seven Hills the way it's always been. Successful. Lush. Home."

When Rick said nothing, she stopped walking and caught his arm forcing him to stop, too. "I need for you to understand this. I'm not taking this job because I want to play at being an entrepreneur or business-woman or horseperson of the year. I want to keep my home my home."

He studied her for a few seconds then said, "I understand that."

"Do you?"

"Yes. I didn't come home only because I needed help with Ruthie. I came home because I like the peace and quiet of Calhoun Corners. If at all possible, I want to raise my daughter here. I want my dad reelected so we don't have to worry that the town's going to change overnight. So, yeah, I understand exactly what you're saying."

"So we agree."

He shrugged. "Yes. We do agree. Again. Not only do we both do the right thing when pushed, but we both understand home." He started walking to the barn. "But for now our job is only to make sure Sweet Potato really is the horse that we want. If he checks out then we take him with us when we go."

"Sounds good to me."

The whole transaction took less than two hours. Rick approved the horse, then handed a certified check to the owner. They loaded Sweet Potato into the trailer and drove back to Seven Hills.

As Rick turned the stallion over to Toby, his cell phone rang. He glanced down at the caller ID and, letting the phone ring again, faced Toby. "You and Sweet Potato go on without me, Toby. I may be a minute."

Not quite sure what Rick wanted her to do since he hadn't included her in on his instructions to Toby, Ashley stayed beside his truck as he answered his ringing phone.

"Hey, Mom, what's up?" He paused, listening, then frowned. "Okay." Another pause. This time as he listened he grimaced. "Okay. Sure. I understand."

He snapped his phone closed, then sighed as he caught Ashley's gaze. "I really wanted to go over a couple more things with you, but Tia had a doctor's appointment this afternoon which she forgot about. So she called my mother who had no choice but to bring Ruthie to my house to watch her there."

"So Ruthie's home?"

"Yes. Unfortunately my mother can't stay any longer. She needs to get back to her own house to make dinner for my dad. But she made me supper. Fried chicken. If you want, you could come to the guesthouse with me to talk a bit more about the record-keeping, vendors, that kind of stuff. And I could feed you."

"Real food?"

"Don't you have a cook or something?"

"We have a housekeeper, but she only comes in three times a week. She doesn't cook."

"What do you eat?"

Ashley shrugged. "I cook. But since I've been working twelve to sixteen hours a day this week, I haven't had time for much more than frozen dinners. Last night when Rayne parked beside me at the counter of the diner, I ended up leaving half my stew."

"Did you get lunch?"

"A sandwich."

He shook his head. "Come on. Let's go."

They hopped into Rick's truck and drove the short distance to the guesthouse. After pulling into the parking space beside the little Cape Cod, Rick cut the engine and reached for his door handle. "I never guessed when you discovered Ruthie that it would actually come in handy."

"Yeah," Ashley said, jumping out of the truck. "But you really only have about another week to hide her."

"Ten days," Rick agreed, climbing the steps. He pulled open the screen door and called, "Mom, we're here."

Holding Ruthie, Elizabeth all but ran from the kitchen to the front foyer. "Great." She handed the baby to Rick. "Sorry about this, but I have to get the heck home and make dinner for your dad."

"It's not a problem," Rick said, smiling when Ruthie

nuzzled her nose into his shirt collar. "Ashley and I have to go over a few things. We can do it here as easily as in her dad's den."

As if only noticing Ashley, Elizabeth said, "Oh, Ashley's here. Great." She said, "Hi, Ashley," then ran to the door, shoved it open and was across the porch and down the steps before Ashley could count to three.

Ashley laughed. "Does she always run when she knows your dad's about to come home?"

"Yes," Rick said, leading Ashley into the kitchen and toward the wonderful scent of fried chicken. "But not because he's bossy. Because she likes him."

Waving at Ruthie, who was peering at her over Rick's shoulder, Ashley followed Rick into the kitchen. "Really?"

"Yeah. They genuinely like each other." He shook his head. "When my brother and I were younger, and they would kiss each other or jump to please each other, Jericho and I would make gagging noises and mutter about how disgusting they were. Now, I wish I could find a relationship like they have."

Ashley laughed. "You like all the smooshy, gushing, mushy stuff?"

"Yeah," he said, sounding surprised that she didn't. "Because it's not about romance or sex with them. The kissing and hugging and catering to each other is a sign of their commitment."

Ashley turned and peered out the screen door, catching a glimpse of Elizabeth's taillights as she roared out of the lane. "And that's what you want?"

He sighed. "Actually, Ashley, it doesn't matter. I'm

not going to find what my parents have because I'm not going to look for it. I have a child, who is the grand-daughter of a senator who's technically living a double life. So for me all the rules have changed. I won't drag another person into my mess." He paused in the kitchen doorway. "I forgot her baby seat. Would you get it?"

Having already concluded that the only reason he would run would be if Ruthie were threatened, Ashley didn't comment on what he'd said and focused on his request that she get the baby seat. She said, "Okay," then darted back into the living room to grab the baby chair. She brought it to the kitchen and glanced around, not sure what to do. "Where do I put it?"

"Just put it on the table."

When Ashley had done as he suggested, Rick slid Ruthie into the seat. "I give her a side of the table and I take the other side. This way she gets to have dinner with me and I don't have to worry that she'll put her foot in my potatoes."

Ashley laughed.

"You laugh." Rick snapped the safety harness of Ruthie's seat. "But just wait until you see how she can jump and sputter and make her presence known." He turned away from the table and pointed at the covered platter on the stove. "That's probably the chicken. Mom said potato salad is in the refrigerator. There's a gallon of iced tea in there, too."

"Yum."

"Plates are in the cabinet beside the stove, so grab a plate and some chicken while I get the tea and the potato salad."

Ashley put two pieces of chicken on her plate and two pieces of chicken on a second plate for Rick. She set them on the table then went back to the cupboard for glasses. By the time she sat, Rick had retrieved the iced tea and the potato salad. As Rick poured their beverages, Ashley scooped a spoonful of potato salad onto her plate, then one onto his.

"Okay, now we're set," Rick said, putting a rattle into Ruthie's hand. She banged it against her chubby little thigh with a yelp.

"When she yelps like that I always feel like she's trying to convince me she's old enough for solid food."

Ashley chuckled. "If she can smell this, she probably is." She took a bite of her chicken and groaned in ecstasy. "Oh Lord this is good."

"I thought you said you could cook?"

"There's cooking and then there's *cooking*. This is obviously the fried chicken of someone with decades of experience."

"Yeah, my mom's good," Rick agreed, but before he took a second bite of chicken he changed the subject. "So, what did you think of the records you reviewed this morning?"

"I think we need to extend our vendor list."

He pondered that as he chewed a mouthful of chicken, then said, "There's a loyalty factor to be considered. Because Calhoun Corners is a small town, the surrounding farms support certain businesses like the hardware store. We consistently buy from them so they know they can depend upon us. If we stop supporting them, or distribute our hardware business among several vendors, Bert's revenues could slip and he could decide to close up shop."

"Good point."

With Ruthie happily chewing her rattle, they talked about vendors and accounting while they ate the chicken and potato salad and also discovered a chocolate cake that Rick's mother had obviously made but forgotten to mention.

After each had eaten a piece of cake, they took Ruthie to her nursery and Rick initiated a discussion of races, as he bathed the little girl. Ruthie splashed and sang and Rick occasionally paused to talk to her and Ashley watched him. The feeling of happiness she had had in the truck returned and this time Ashley recategorized it. It wasn't happiness. It was more like contentment.

Here she was, on a chilly fall night, sitting on the window seat of a cozy bedroom, watching a dad care for his happy daughter. And she suddenly understood what he had said about his parents. Right at this moment, if he wanted a kiss, she would kiss him. Not because he was gorgeous, though he was. She wanted to kiss him because of something warm and sweet that seemed to encompass so much more than simple attraction. They had reached so many understandings that day. And that was the difference between this relationship and any other she had had. *They'd* reached so many understandings. She hadn't been the only one learning. Rick had been bending, too. He was the first person to really ever understand her.

Or try.

"So, should we continue?" he asked, turning away from the crib after tucking in Ruthie for the night. He motioned for Ashley to leave and walked through the nursery door behind her.

She waited until they were in the hall before she said, "I'm a bit tired."

"It is late," he agreed as they walked down the steps.

Ashley was struck again by how casual they were. How well they got along. How right it felt to be together. They reached the bottom of the stairs and she turned to face him. "I think I'll just get going."

He smiled. "Okay. See you in the morning."

But Ashley didn't move. He had expressive blue eyes that flashed with fire when he was angry, sizzled with attraction when he caught her in compromising positions, and filled with warmth when he was with Ruthie. Right now, they were filled with that warmth. A day's growth of beard darkened his chin and cheeks. Solid muscle filled out his workshirt. He was an incredibly attractive man who'd been dealt some of life's toughest cards, yet he hadn't become bitter. In fact, he was kind, generous and fair. So fair she was comfortable with a man for the first time since her horrible marriage.

But she wasn't entirely relaxed. A sexual tension hummed between them. And their "accidental" kiss suddenly felt like unfinished business. It didn't seem right to just leave. In fact, if there was something between them, something real, something right, then she wanted it.

She took a step closer. He didn't move. She smiled, but rather than return her smile, the warm expression in his eyes shifted to confusion. She didn't blame him for being confused. The last thing she had expected was that they would fit. But they did.

She stretched toward him and in the final second before she pressed her lips to his she closed her eyes. Sensation sizzled through her, but not just from sexual chemistry. The knowledge that they fit made her bold, curious. What would it be like to be involved with a man who didn't hesitate to teach her, to consider her an equal, to love her for real, not just for her money?

Putting her hands on Rick's shoulders, Ashley stepped closer, deepening the kiss. At first she thought Rick would resist, but his hands slowly came to her waist, even as his mouth opened over hers. The thought that she could be his equal came to her again, but not in the sense that they would be work partners or even friends, but sexual equals. This was a man who would expect a woman to hold her own in bed and suddenly she realized she wanted to. She wanted to give him everything she had, everything she could be, if he would simply let her open up.

His hands at her waist nudged her closer. Her arms tightened around his neck until her breasts were flattened against his chest and their thighs were pressed together intimately. A hunger thrummed between them and she realized how desperate she'd been for this minute, for this man.

He broke the kiss, backed off. "This isn't right."

But the look in his eyes didn't match his words. Breathless with yearning, Ashley stared at him, knowing there was something between them, something that mixed friendship with passion. Something that felt as if it could be very important to both of them. Maybe the most important relationship of their lives. She absolutely could not give this up.

Rather than back away, she kissed him again, not sure if she was testing her instincts or his resolve, and again felt the spiral of arousal that she hadn't felt in four long years. Though other men had attracted her, none had deserved her trust. That was the key.

When she pulled back, their lips parted reluctantly, and she knew that even if he didn't feel the incredible emotion that simmered inside her, he felt the passion. He stepped away from it only with hesitation.

Holding his gaze, she softly said, "It sure as heck feels right to me."

"And in some ways it feels right to me," he admitted equally quietly. "Different. I know you understand me because you've gone through a lot of the same things I have. You've been the object of the town's gossip, and you even embarrassed and angered your dad when you lost half your trust fund, the way I embarrassed and angered my dad with my pranks through high school."

"You're such a sweet-talker."

He laughed. "That's another thing. I'm not afraid to say what I mean with you."

This time she laughed.

Drawing in a long drink of air, he stepped away. "You think what I'm saying is funny or foolish but it's not. With you I have the thing that was missing with Jen. Total acceptance. And tonight that's a stronger aphrodisiac than the way you looked in that little pink thing the day I dragged you out of bed."

"I've never had anybody who understood me, either…"

"Ashley, don't." This time his voice was a desperate whisper. "I don't have anything to offer you. More than that, I don't know what's going to happen with Senator Martin." He took a breath. "Jen told me some things about her dad, including that her mom had to sign a non-disclosure agreement when they divorced. There's only one reason for that. He did things he's ashamed of. Even if I didn't want to raise my own child, I couldn't risk that he got custody."

"What are you saying?"

"I'm saying that if it looked like Senator Martin was about to be awarded custody of my child, I would leave. Run."

"I know that."

"And I wouldn't take you with me. I wouldn't ask you to leave your home. I wouldn't ask you to give up ever being able to contact your dad again. I couldn't risk that somehow you could be the link that would allow a private investigator or law enforcement to find us."

He ran his fingertips across her chin, though, as if he were sorely tempted to kiss her again, and Ashley knew that if she kissed him again, he probably wouldn't turn her away. They'd end up in his bed because whatever it was that pulsed between them, it was powerful.

And she wasn't surprised that he would run to protect his daughter. She'd already figured that out. What surprised her was that he didn't trust her. He was the first man she'd trusted in years and he didn't return her trust. Worse, she wasn't entirely sure he ever could. Not because she wasn't trustworthy, but because he had been burned. And this time around she wanted somebody who could love her. Totally. Passionately. A person couldn't love her the way she wanted to be loved, if he didn't trust her.

So she walked out of the guesthouse without even a goodbye. There was no sense dissecting their situation anymore, and she didn't want him to see how much his rejection hurt her.

Chapter Seven

The next morning Ashley dressed in a pantsuit, swept her hair up into a ponytail and took a thermal cup of coffee to the barn office, along with a carafe filled with the coffee that had remained in her pot. When Toby walked in, he whistled.

"Wow. You look great."

"And I brought coffee."

"That's part of the reason you look great," Toby said with a grin as he held out his half-empty cup, looking for a warm-up.

Ashley laughed and filled his cup at the same time that Rick entered the barn. She glanced over just as he looked at her and their gazes caught and held.

After two hours of tossing and turning the night before, Ashley had decided he'd been right. He didn't know her well enough to trust her, let alone ask her to run with him if he needed to leave to protect Ruthie.

But there was another side to that coin. She didn't know *him* well enough to say with certainty that she wanted to give up the farm, her dad, her friends, her life, to hide with him. Not that she thought they would have to go on the run. If they were together, he'd have access to enough money to fight Senator Martin. And if they had a relationship, they would manage the farm together. And as comanager of Seven Hills he would have the respectability that would keep him from losing a custody battle.

But that actually took them to the real barrier of their situation. If she made him comanager she would never really know if he was falling in love with her for her, or because she made his life easier. Worse, if she offered him the job as comanager, he might leave rather than take it, if only because he refused to be called an opportunist. After the way she had fought for the job, he would know she was only offering it to get him to stay and he wouldn't let himself be trapped into the identity he'd grown out of.

So they were stuck. Caught. There was no way to work this out.

To break the oppressive silence, Ashley said, "I brought coffee."

Rick raised his cup of store-bought. "I have my own, thanks."

"Great." Cool and nonchalant, she glanced around the little room, hoping to show him that there were no hard feelings and things could be normal and easy between them. "I was thinking that we should get a cof-feemaker for in here."

Rick shook his head. "If you buy a coffeemaker, you have to buy coffee. It isn't a one-time expense."

"I'm okay with that."

Toby hooted with laughter. "I might just like having a girl in charge."

"I'm not in charge yet."

Toby brushed off her concern. "You will be when your dad retires."

"*When* my dad retires," Ashley reminded Toby firmly. "I don't want you to go around spreading rumors that he's retiring."

Again, Toby brushed her off with a dismissive wave of his hand. "The rumor's already out."

"So, let's not fuel the fire." She turned to Rick. "What do you have for us to do today?"

"More of what we did yesterday." He reached across the desk and picked up a clipboard. "How was Sweet Potato last night?" he asked Toby.

"Slept like a baby."

"Okay, then. You take care of him this morning. I'll sneak a peek at him sometime this afternoon. Right now Ashley and I are going to go up to the house and jump back into the books."

Toby said, "Sounds good to me," then he nodded at the carafe Ashley still held. "You might want to leave that coffee."

Ashley smiled. "Sure."

Ashley and Rick left the barn and walked to her house in silence. She stripped off her suit jacket and hung it on the newel post in the foyer as they passed it on their way to the den.

Stepping into the dark room, Rick flipped the light switch and pointed at the seat behind the desk. "You get the position of honor."

"Thanks."

She sat in the tall-backed office chair, turned on the lamp, and pressed the button for the computer monitor.

Rick leaned his hip on the corner of the desk. "They really like you, you know."

She turned to face him. "Who?"

"All the guys in the barn."

He made the observation without emotion, but holding the gaze of his pretty blue eyes, Ashley knew he was talking about more than the employees of Seven Hills. He liked her, too. He seemed to be saying that he was sorry that things couldn't be different between them.

She was, too, but she also knew that if he wanted to have a discussion of their relationship, he'd come right out and say what was on his mind. Using backhanded communication was his way of telling her that he regretted the way things had to be but he didn't want to belabor something that couldn't be resolved with another discussion. She respected his wishes by keeping her reply in the same venue as his comment.

"It's good to know I have their support."

"With your brains and their support, you'll do very, very well."

Without him.

More backhanded communication. Turning her attention to the computer, she smiled sadly to herself as she used the mouse to start the program she needed. It was sweet of him to reassure her, but she didn't need his reassurance, when it came to almost having things and recovering from the wanting, she was an expert.

"I always do."

"Just don't get cocky."

That made her laugh. Again, he didn't have to warn her. She knew better than to get presumptuous about anything in her life. She'd lost her mother and brother to an accident, her husband to greed and now her dad to retirement. Once her dad returned, even Rick would leave. Nobody stayed in her life.

They worked until eleven, when Rick announced they needed to go into town.

"Why?"

"Randy Dupont is meeting us for lunch at the diner."

"My dad's accountant?"

He nodded. "After that we're going across the street to meet with Frank Barnes."

She whistled. "Both the accountant and attorney in the same day."

"When I say I'm going to do something, I do it. You need to be in good standing with the people who provide professional advice to your dad and by default the farm. You need to know what they do, but more than that you need to establish trust."

"I do trust them."

He laughed. "*They* need to trust *you*."

"And how do I accomplish that?"

"You have breakfast, lunch or dinner with them every

few weeks and in casual conversation you tell them what you're doing at the farm. Eventually they'll either decide you're a safe bet or they'll tell your dad he should look elsewhere for a replacement."

She gaped at him, but before she could say anything he said, "You'll be fine. You won me over." He laid his hand on his chest for emphasis. "And I wanted the job. When your dad gets home in February, you're going to knock his socks off. Not just because you know everything that's going on, but because you've won over the people most important to him. The guy who keeps track of his money and the guy who keeps him out of trouble."

Ashley smiled. "Thanks."

"You're welcome." He turned and began walking out of the den. Ashley scrambled after him, grabbing her jacket off the newel post in the foyer and following him out of the house.

When they stepped out onto the front porch she said, "We'll take my SUV."

"I don't mind driving."

"I know, but I'm getting accustomed to being the boss."

He chuckled and motioned for her to lead the way to her SUV. "You like being in the driver's seat."

"Very much. It's fun to be in control."

He gave her a smoldering look that sent her blood racing, but quickly turned away and rounded the hood of her SUV, entering on the passenger's side. Ashley took a long breath before she opened her door. It was always going to be like this between them. Their chemistry could turn even the most innocent comment into something sexual. The air between them could go from casual to sizzling with the drop of a wrong word. But that was part of their problem. If they continued to spend so much time in each other's company, they were absolutely going to end up sleeping together. Then the decision to forget about having any kind of permanent relationship, which had been difficult the night before, would be impossible. Worse, one of them or both of them would end up being hurt.

At lunch with the accountant and the meeting with her father's attorney, Rick introduced Ashley as the person being groomed to take over Seven Hills and neither man batted an eye, but both subtly grilled her. In what appeared to be lunch conversation Randy Dupont asked questions designed to ferret out her education. Later that afternoon, Ashley's father's attorney asked questions that had more to do with her understanding of things that might potentially get her sued. It was a long afternoon, but a productive afternoon. Though Ashley hadn't precisely bowled over her dad's advisors, she absolutely felt she'd passed a few first tests.

Their positive reactions to her filled her with so much confidence that when she and Rick returned to Seven Hills a little after four, and Rick excused himself to pay a visit to Sweet Potato followed by a visit to Ruthie, Ashley waved goodbye and rushed back to the den to call her father.

Falling into the padded leather chair behind the big desk, she grabbed the receiver for the phone and dialed his cell phone number from memory. A woman answered, probably a new maid who didn't know her father hated for anyone to touch his cell, and not wanting to get in the middle of *that* argument, Ashley only said, "Hi, I'm calling for Mr. Meljac."

"I'm sorry he's not here right now."

Imagining her father going anywhere without his phone confused Ashley so much, her brow furrowed. "And he didn't take his cell?"

"He's swimming."

"Oh. Okay. I get it. Can I leave a message?"

"Sure, let me get my mom to take that."

"Your mom?"

"She's Gene's fiancée. She's better with messages than I am."

Because Ashley's brain froze on the word fiancée, she hardly heard the second half of that sentence. It made so little sense to think her dad was engaged that the only logical explanation she could think of was that the maid's daughter liked to play games.

"Hello?"

Ashley took a steadying breath. "Hi. With whom am I speaking, please?"

"Mr. Meljac's fiancée. Who is this?"

Ashley couldn't immediately reply because her breath caught and her heart stopped. Her dad was engaged? There had to be some kind of mistake.

"Gene's not here right now and my daughter told me you needed to leave a message. Do you need to leave a message?"

"Actually I think I'll call back."

As if realizing she might have been too abrupt, Ashley's dad's fiancée softened her tone. "I can take a message."

Ashley swallowed. Her dad had done a lot of secret things in his life, but even he wouldn't keep a fiancée secret from her. This had to be a misunderstanding.

Forcing herself to calm down, she said, "Tell Mr. Meljac his daughter called. And that he might want to call me back."

There was a short pause at the other end of the line, then her father's fiancée said, "Let me get him from the pool."

Rick spent over an hour with Sweet Potato, then raced to Tia's for his quick visit with Ruthie. When he walked into Tia's house, he heard Ruthie's wails coming from the kitchen and he headed back that way.

"Hey, what's going on?" he asked as he pushed open the swinging door and walked in.

Pacing the kitchen floor as she rocked Rick's little girl, Tia said, "I think she's teething. Mom's on her way."

"Here. Let me take her," Rick said reaching for the sobbing baby. Wearing a ruffle-skirted pink dress with a pink ribbon tied in her wisp of black hair, Ruthie looked cute enough to model baby clothes. Rick kissed her forehead as he snuggled her to his shoulder. "What's up, kitten?"

She sniffled, rubbing her wet nose in his shirt collar and Tia laughed.

Rick sighed. "I have no idea why she does that to me, but she's always wiping her nose on my shirt."

"Maybe she likes your scent?"

That explanation was so darned much nicer than the ones Rick had imagined that he chuckled and glanced down at his baby girl. To his amazement, Ruthie wasn't crying anymore. Because she'd rubbed her little face in his shirt, her tears were dry. Only her swollen eyes remained.

Tia smiled affectionately. "Or maybe she just likes you?"

Rick's heart melted with love. "Do you realize that this is the first time she's preferred me over a woman?"

Tia laughed. "You're making that up."

"Has she ever cried—any morning—when I dropped her off with you?" Not waiting for an answer, Rick said, "No. She hasn't. She's never wanted *me* before. This is a first."

"Well, it's a good first."

"And it also means I'm not going back to work. If I'm the only person she wants right now," he said, feeling his heart swell with love again, and also with the hope that maybe he was going to be a passable dad after all, "then I need to be with her."

"Do you want me to call Ashley?"

"No," Rick said, reaching into his jeans pocket for his cell phone. "I have her number," he said pushing the button that connected it for him.

Tia laughed. "Really? Is there something I should know about going on between the two of you?"

"Yeah, in the beginning of our acquaintance I was trying to annoy her so much she would realize she didn't want to be a farm manager. But she took everything I could dish out and more and I decided she deserves the job and I'm training her for real."

As Rick heard Ashley's answering machine come on, Tia said, "Oh, Rick, this job is so perfect for you. I can't believe you're giving it up."

"It was never mine. Gene hired me temporarily. I had hoped to prove myself while he was away, so he would offer it to me permanently when he retires. But when he comes back in February, he'll see that Ashley's ready to take over. I'm sure he'll make her manager in the summer when he leaves to sail around the world and officially retires."

Tia shook her head. "It's hard to believe a guy who is only in his mid-forties wants to retire."

Rick shrugged. "I wouldn't exactly say he's retiring. From the conversations I've had with him I've gathered that he's tired of farming. He loves the islands now. Sailing especially. I think what he's doing is slowing down so he can enjoy the fruits of all his hard work." When Ashley's answering machine recording was finished, Rick decided against leaving a message and snapped his cell phone closed.

Tia nodded, then said, "You aren't going to leave a message?"

"No, I want to talk to Ashley personally. I know she's there so she was probably in the middle of changing or something and couldn't get to the phone. I'll wait a minute and call again."

But there was no answer the second time Rick called. Or the third. After his fourth attempt, he took a seat at the kitchen table, and entertained both Ruthie and Tia as he let fifteen minutes go by before he tried a fifth time.

His mother arrived as he was closing his cell phone and she immediately walked over and took Ruthie from his lap.

"She looks fine."

"Trust me, Mom," Tia said. "She was wailing up a

small storm before Rick got here. Something was definitely wrong."

Elizabeth tilted her head, studying the baby. "She could be teething, or she might have just missed her daddy." She smiled at Rick. "You want to take her again?"

As much as Rick wanted to bask in the joy of finally having parental acceptance from Ruthie, he also had a bad feeling about Ashley not answering her phone. Especially since she was alone in her house. She could fall and hurt herself, and no one would find her until she didn't show up for work the next morning.

He rose from his seat at the kitchen table. "Actually it doesn't seem right that I can't reach Ashley. I've called five times and she won't pick up."

"Maybe she's not home."

"I was supposed to come back to Seven Hills and go over a few more things. I know she's eager to learn so it doesn't make sense that she'd leave. I'm surprised she hasn't tried to call me to find out what's taking me so long."

He took Ruthie from his mother for one last quick kiss, then handed her back and headed for the door. When he turned to say goodbye he was relieved to notice that Ruthie seemed perfectly content with her grandmother.

Nonetheless, he said, "I won't stay long. I want to get back to Ruthie. I'll just be gone enough to make sure everything's okay and explain that I need to be with Ruthie tonight."

Tia waved him on. "Take as long as you want. Ruthie seems fine now. Not only that, but I wasn't expecting you until after eight, so I was planning to teach Drew to change diapers."

Rick laughed and left Tia's house. He hopped into his truck and drove to the main house at Seven Hills. As he approached, he saw that lights were on in the front foyer and kitchen, the same lights he and Ashley had probably turned on when they'd arrived that afternoon, but the light in the den was off. Which probably meant she was making herself something for supper.

Hoping she was making enough for two, he jogged up the front porch steps and rang the bell but there was no answer. He knocked, but, again, no answer.

His instincts kicked into overdrive. He didn't think Ashley was crushed by their mutual decision the night before not to pursue a relationship. After all, they'd really only known each other a few days. So it wasn't as if either one of them had broken the other's heart. Though they did have a powerful attraction and there were so damned many reasons he'd love to be more than just the guy teaching her how to run her farm. She was gorgeous. She was smart. She liked Ruthie. And she just plain made him laugh.

But he accepted that their circumstances didn't allow for them to pursue the attraction, and he knew she was smart enough to accept it, too. With her SUV in the driveway, not put away for the night in the garage, the sun nearly set and lights on in her house, Rick couldn't think of a good reason she wouldn't answer the phone or the door.

And the explanation that jumped to mind was that she *couldn't* answer the door. She might have hurt herself or been hurt by an intruder. He twisted the knob but the front door was locked. So he walked around back to the kitchen door, which he hadn't locked when he left that afternoon. He tried it and it was open.

He entered her kitchen calling, "Ashley!"

She didn't answer so he peeked into the laundry room/bathroom area and didn't see her. He walked through the kitchen and into the long corridor that led to the formal dining room. Still no Ashley.

In the foyer, he called up the steps, "Ashley! Ash! Are you home?"

When he received no answer to his call, he turned to the left. A slim light at the back of the hall leading to the den caught Rick's attention and he headed down that corridor. When he reached the den door, he saw that the desk lamp was on. It had provided just enough light to draw him back into the hall and now illuminated Ashley sitting at the desk in the otherwise dark room.

He stepped into the room. "Hey. What's up?"

She didn't answer.

He flipped the switch that turned on the overhead lights and saw the totally blank expression on her face.

"Ashley?" he said, walking across the yellowish rug to the mahogany desk. "Are you okay?"

She swallowed. "Did you know?"

"Know what?"

"Of course, you did." She leaned back on the tall-backed chair and sighed. "That's why you took this job. You knew it would become permanent sooner rather than later. You might have even been gambling that my dad wouldn't come home from this trip at all."

He took another few steps toward the desk. "What are you talking about?"

"My dad's engagement."

Totally confused now, Rick said, "What engagement?"

"My dad's engaged to some woman who lives with him in his condo on the island."

Though he understood how it would hurt Ashley, Rick wasn't all that surprised by the news that Gene had found another woman.

"Ash, your dad's only in his forties. That's awful young to be without a companion."

"Yeah," she replied casually, rising from the seat behind the desk and rounding the corner to leave. "I guess the job of running the farm really is mine. I'll see you in the morning. Right now I just want to be alone."

He should have let her go. He shouldn't have felt the pain of betrayal he knew she felt, but he did. He knew what it was like to think you knew somebody, only to have that person do something to prove you didn't understand him or her at all. He also knew what it was like to be dumped. Left. Forgotten. Though Ashley's dad hadn't dumped her, he'd clearly shut her out of his life.

As Ashley tried to breeze by the desk, Rick caught her arm to stop her. "Hey. Come on. This is me. I know you're mad. Hell, you were mad when you thought your dad was retiring and hadn't confided that to you."

Her chin came up.

"But you got beyond that by being tough. You stay tough and you'll end up okay."

"This isn't like him keeping his retirement a secret. His job and this farm and his money have always been things he kept private. Getting engaged without telling your family is personal." She shook her head as if frustrated. "No, this goes beyond my dad being engaged. The girl who answered the phone said that her mother was my dad's fiancé. From the sounds of things, he has an entire family down there."

"And you have an entire family here."

"I have a farm and employees."

"This morning that was good enough."

She squeezed her eyes shut and Rick's heart ached for her, but he said nothing.

"He invited me down for the holidays. He wants me to meet "everybody" and I will go down. But I know how this will turn out. Even if everybody loves me and I love them, I'll forever be an outsider because the family was formed without me. He did all this *without* me! And he's not apologetic. He said he never believed it would get this far this fast and by the time he realized it had it was too late to bring me into the loop." Furious, she pounded her bunched fists against Rick's shoulder. "Into the loop. That's what he said. Like I was a damned business partner!"

She burst into tears and Rick pulled her into his arms, purely to comfort her. At first that was all he did. He stroked her hair, and let her cry, while whispering things that sometimes didn't make any sense. Because if there was one thing he had learned over the years it was that sometimes life didn't make any sense. Ashley was twenty-six, old enough to be on her own, but she'd lost her mother and brother, then she'd been cheated by a selfish husband, so she appreciated the comfort and safety of family. At the same time, her dad probably felt he was being held back. Gene may have even felt torn in two. Wanting to get on with his life, he'd found a new love, but not wanting to hurt Ashley he hadn't told her.

"If you really think this through," Rick said, holding Ashley against his shoulder, "your dad has waited long enough to move on."

She said nothing.

"And you're not a little girl anymore." Rick didn't know if he was doing the right thing, but what he was saying was the truth. And though painful, sometimes the truth was the only way out of a bad situation. "You're an adult, who shouldn't need him."

He felt her stiffen.

"You know it's true."

She took a breath, then relaxed as if what he'd said had stung at first, but she recognized the truth of it and had begun to accept it.

"Besides, if the tables were turned what would you do?"

When she said nothing, he pushed her away just slightly so he could see the look on her face. Her eyes brimmed with tears, but she wasn't crying anymore.

Finally she whispered, "My dad never met Thad until after I married him."

"Do you think keeping his engagement quiet was payback?"

She shook her head. "No. He told me tonight on the phone that the whole romance just happened. Almost as if it fell out of the sky for him." She smiled sadly. "As obtuse as my dad is sometimes about feelings, I actually believe that."

"So you're not mad?"

"I was never mad. I was hurt."

Rick softened his voice. "I know."

"The worst of it is, I don't want to be. He is young. He does deserve a whole new wonderful life. I just wanted to be part of it, too."

"And leave the farm? The job you've wanted forever? The people you had hoped to turn into family?"

Rick watched her expression change as she considered that. "I guess I have been a little obsessive about the farm."

"A little."

"So he may have held back on telling me about his new life on the islands because he knew how I felt about keeping Seven Hills a home." She shook her head sadly. "He may have even thought I'd try to talk him out of it."

Rick shrugged. "Or maybe he didn't tell you because having you manage Seven Hills means he gets to keep both of his homes. I don't think he wanted to leave the farm, either, Ashley. At least not permanently. But from the way he spoke when he interviewed me, I could tell he didn't believe his future was here. Not the way you do."

"Yeah." Her crying now completely stopped, Ashley took a cleansing breath and smiled up at him.

Rick's heart flopped over in his chest. His natural affection for Ashley had completely obliterated his common sense and he'd comforted her before he thought the whole situation through. And for his trouble he'd ended up closer to her than he was allowed to be. Not just physically, but emotionally. He wanted to step back, to step away, even to leave, but somehow his feet weren't getting the message.

She whispered, "Thanks."

His heart melted the same way it had when he'd realized Ruthie wanted *him* that afternoon. But as quickly as Rick recognized how much he was growing to care for Ashley, his emotions shifted and changed. Men weren't built to feel only warm cuddly things for women. When they crossed a certain threshold of affection, hormones got involved, nerves came to life, skin began to tingle with need and desires turned dark and sensual.

He swallowed.

She smiled again and he didn't even try to resist. He leaned forward and touched his lips to hers. She slid her arms around him as naturally as breathing and Rick let his instincts take control. Slowly, as if they had all the time in the world, he slid his mouth across her mouth, tasting, testing, before he opened his lips over hers and let her make the choice of whether they deepened the kiss.

She did and for Rick the world spun crazily. But even though he could have kissed her forever, he remembered that a relationship between them was impossible. She was struggling enough with the emotions of letting her dad go. Rick knew it would kill her if he were to step in now when she needed him, begin to create the home she wanted, and then leave because Senator Martin came after Ruthie.

He found it harder to pull away than the other times they had kissed, but he did.

"I gotta go," he whispered, though everything inside of him was telling him to stay.

"Stay."

He shook his head and tried to step back, but she grabbed his arm.

"I *can't* stay."

"Please."

"No!" He said it violently this time because he knew she didn't understand that she was pulling him in two, making him want something he couldn't have. And not just because he didn't want her to be hurt. He didn't want to be hurt, either. "Don't you get it? I want this."

"Is that so bad?"

"Yes. Even if I didn't have Ruthie, in February I would still be leaving."

"What if you weren't?"

He shook his head sadly. "Ashley, say I did find a job here in Calhoun Corners and that we started to date and even fell in love. Then picture yourself waking up one morning to find me gone because Senator Martin filed for custody of Ruthie. Because that's exactly what's going to happen. Someday, he will find her and when he does I'll be gone because I'll never beat him in a custody battle."

She licked her lips, then quietly said, "You could if you had enough money."

"I wouldn't lose Ruthie because I'm poor. I'd lose because I spent the last ten years of my life bumming around, risking my life, indulging my fantasies. I might be able to tell you that I've changed and have you believe me because you also made a mistake, got burned and realized you couldn't continue living the way you were. So you know the right mistake can change a person in the blink of an eye. But Senator Martin's attorneys wouldn't buy it for a second. They wouldn't *want* to buy it. They'd use it to rip me to smithereens."

"Not if you had enough character witnesses. I'm sure you could prove…"

"Damn it, Ashley! I couldn't! But even if I could, you should want more than this," he said, pointing at his chest. "You don't know me. You think you do but you don't. And until you do you can't go making big decisions like sleeping with me, finding me character witnesses and giving me the money to fight for Ruthie."

He rubbed his hand along the back of his neck then headed for the door. "Someday you're going to find a man who deserves you and when you do, you'll thank me for leaving."

He strode out of the den knowing she was watching him go, knowing she was alone, knowing that she believed she would be alone for the rest of her life.

But she wouldn't and that was why he had to be the strong one. His greater life experience made it easy for him to see that she was a beautiful, intelligent woman. Once she was introduced to the world as the manager, someday-to-be-owner of Seven Hills, she would attract men with money and power. She'd attract the kind of man she deserved.

Chapter Eight

Standing alone in her father's den, Ashley wasn't as upset as Rick thought, mostly because she didn't agree that they couldn't have a personal relationship. After the way he had talked her through her difficult situation that night, it was very clear to her that they were perfectly matched. But she also knew her emotional state about her dad might have skewed her opinions. So for over a week, she said nothing personal to Rick. She let the days go by with them simply interacting as mutually respectful coworkers. She recognized that she had to accustom herself to her father's engagement and get her emotions to a normal level before she drew conclusions about anything. She also wanted some time to watch Rick.

But she didn't need as long as she thought to recognize that her original observations were correct. In one week Rick's interactions with the farm workers, his daughter and even Ashley herself proved he was good, kind, smart, fair. And she was tired of waiting, tired of being alone, especially when someone so perfect was just a touch away and the opportunity to show him how she felt was at hand.

The party's annual preelection dinner wasn't held at the fire hall as Calhoun Corners's local meetings and receptions typically were. This dinner, the biggest event of the year, was held at a fancy hotel in Charlottesville. Ashley had been to it with her dad every year since her mother died. She didn't feel odd that she wasn't going with her father that year. After the initial shock of her dad's engagement had worn off, Ashley knew Rick was right. Her dad was too young to be alone and it was time for her to get on with the rest of her life.

In fact, dressing for dinner that night, she had begun to look forward to moving on because she now had a purpose. A mission. Rick was the most honest, most genuine man she had ever met and she wanted him. No, she didn't *want* him; she loved him. Nobody had ever cared for her the way he had the night she'd heard about her father's engagement. He hadn't babied her. He'd been honest with her, but he'd done it kindly. And even with a bit of humor. He was strong, but he had a soft heart. She needed his honesty, loved how he couldn't stand to see her hurt, needed his help with the farm, and wanted to be a mother to his desperate-for-female-attention baby girl.

She didn't believe it was an accident that he'd come to her father for a job. She knew it was fate. In less than two weeks, she'd not only realized how well they fit, but she'd fallen in love and now she had to convince Rick they could make this work.

Finished dressing for the preelection dinner, Ashley studied her reflection in the full-length mirror with a critical eye. Having attended this event every year for the past four, she knew how well she could dress without going overboard and she intended to take advantage of the opportunity.

Her straight, midnight-blue dress looked conservative and demure, but it had absolutely no back. So when they danced, and she would see to it that they would, he would touch her. Not her dress, but her skin. Not in a vulgar way, but in an enticing, tempting way. Just the way she wanted.

She hurried down the steps at the same time that her front doorbell rang. She pulled it open and Rick smiled at her. "Hey you look nice."

She agreed. She did look "nice" from the front view of her simple blue dress, but from the back she was nothing but naughty. He on the other hand looked magnificent. This party wasn't a tuxedo affair. The gentlemen guests wore their best suits and Rick looked fabulous in his. Black with a white shirt and silver tie, his outfit made the most of his dark hair and blue eyes. And it was a struggle not to kiss him.

But he didn't yet realize they were meant to be together, so she couldn't jump in and do the things she wanted to do. More than that, she wasn't just any woman pursuing him. She was an heiress and he was sensitive about being called an opportunist. In the same way that a trainer had to properly bring along a prize stallion, Ashley had to ease Rick into her life correctly or she would spook him. So she took a quick breath and only smiled at him, knowing she had some wonderful subtle tricks up her sleeve—and absolutely no back to her dress.

"I'm ready. Just let me grab my purse," she said, pivoting to snatch the little blue evening bag from the table in the foyer, "and I'll be all set."

When she turned again, the expression on Rick's face was priceless. She gave him an innocent look. "What?"

"Your dress has no back."

"Of course, it has a back," she said, twisting around to glance behind her. She ran her hand along the material that covered her bottom. "See. Everything's covered."

"Everything but your whole damned back! I hope you have a coat. It's November and it's cold out there."

"I have a coat," she said, walking three steps down the hall to the right to retrieve her navy-blue evening coat from the closet. She handed it to him. "Here."

She heard him suck in a breath when she presented her back to him. The very fact that a back wasn't exactly a sexy part of a body gave her several advantages. She didn't appear to be deliberately trying to seduce him. And his consistent reactions to something so innocent proved he was in deeper than he wanted to admit.

With her coat on, she turned and smiled. "Ready?"

"Your car or mine?"

Because she'd thought this through, she pulled a set of keys from the little blue bag. "Let's take Daddy's Mercedes. It's cleaner."

He glanced down at the keys, looking at them as if they would bite him. She knew why. He didn't want people to think he was an opportunist, taking advantage of her or using her for the things in her life. But this was all part of her plan. He needed to get accustomed to all the "things" she and her father owned. He needed to get comfortable with the cars and the big house and the creature comforts. Then, when their attraction turned into a relationship, her things would be a part of his life and no longer an issue.

"Car's in the garage," she said casually and turned quickly, so he didn't notice that she also pulled back the keys. He needed a minute to grow accustomed to taking the car. Which was fine. If push came to shove, she could even drive. This wasn't a date. She'd made arrangements to "ride" together to attend the dinner as employees of the farm attending a dinner to do political glad-handing for the business. She could take this evening as far as Rick would let her.

They walked through the long corridor to the right to enter the multicar garage. Neither said a word as they approached the Mercedes. Two steps before they reached it, Ashley got a brainstorm and said, "Catch," as she tossed the keys at Rick.

He caught them in midair, and glanced over at her. But she quickly looked away, forcing him to either drive or admit he felt uncomfortable. After only a few seconds, he hit the button that unlocked the doors and as if his driving her dad's car were the most ordinary thing in the world, Ashley climbed inside.

The garage door opened automatically when Rick

started the car and closed after they had backed out onto the driveway.

Rick said, "Nice."

"Yeah, money has its advantages."

He snorted a laugh. Then the car got extremely quiet. But Ashley had learned a few lessons from Rick and she didn't intend to break the silence. If she wanted the ball to stay in her court tonight, she had to continue to be casual to the point of being oblivious. That meant having him bring up the obvious first.

"You know everybody's going to think we're together."

Well, that didn't take long. Ashley pretended great interest in something in her purse and said, "Not really. We work together, remember? And we're both going to the dinner tonight to represent the farm's interests. It was smarter to share a ride. If you're worried, we can go our separate ways at the door."

"I'm not going to drive you there and let you sit by yourself."

She smiled down at her lap. He was such a gentleman that he played right into her hands. "Does this mean I get to sit at the mayor's table?"

He shifted uncomfortably on his seat. "I've already mentioned it to my mother. Not because I think you can't handle yourself, but because Tia and Drew decided not to attend."

"It really doesn't matter to me where I sit. I know the organizers don't usually assign seats, so I could mingle with my dad's friends or people trying to get on my good side now that they know I'm going to be running

Seven Hills. Eventually someone will invite me to sit with him," she said, again keeping her voice light, but hoping to stir up a little jealousy before she eased him into phase two of this discussion. "People already know you're training me. Most people will see us as boss and employer." She paused to let that sink in before she added, "Because that's what we are."

"For another couple of months."

Ashley nearly snickered. He was making this incredibly easy. "Actually, Rick, you've hit something that I've been meaning to talk about. I don't really want you to leave when my dad officially retires."

He peered over at her. "Farm doesn't need two managers."

"No, but I wouldn't mind taking over the breeding end of things, and giving everything else to you. Basically you'd be doing everything but nuisance negotiating and scheduling. I'd even want your take on any purchases I decide to make."

When he didn't immediately argue, Ashley knew he was tempted. "You don't have to answer me today. Though your taking a job at Seven Hills permanently would more easily explain our presence tonight. But we don't really need that either because I could sit with any number of people." She shifted on the seat, crossing her ankles to draw his attention to her legs and got exactly the result she wanted.

He looked at her legs. He flexed his fingers on the steering wheel and all but growled his displeasure. "I'd rather you sat with my family, but if you want to sit with someone else that's okay."

"I can't really sit with your family without starting an entire calendar full of gossip." She paused. "Unless we have a bona fide working relationship. Then everybody will see us as representing the interests of Seven Hills."

He drew a quiet breath. "Okay."

Unable to hide her surprise at his easy acquiescence, she peeked at him. "Okay?"

"Yes, I'll work for you after your dad officially retires."

She wanted to shout for joy. If nothing else she wanted to say, "Really?" and hope he gave her a detailed explanation of how they were a good team. Instead she casually said, "Okay."

They walked into the hotel in downtown Charlottesville and Ashley led Rick to the banquet room. "You're mighty familiar with this hotel."

"I attended a lot of banquets with my dad." As soon as they reached the outer hall, Ashley began removing her coat. "Coatroom is down here."

Rick followed her, taking her evening coat from her and handing it across the counter to the attendant, who smiled and gave him a number.

They turned and headed for the open doors of the banquet room. Rick placed his hand on the small of her back, but pulled it off as if it had burned him, shifting it down, only to realize he had settled his hand on her bottom.

"There's nowhere for me to put my hand."

"You could have kept it on my back."

"It wouldn't look right for an employee to have his hand on his employer's naked back."

"Is it better for my employee to have his hand on my butt?"

Rick growled. Ashley laughed. "Come on. Don't put your hand anywhere. You don't have to guide me. I can just lead."

Ashley strode into the banquet room and immediately spotted his father's table. Tall, dark-haired Mayor Capriotti chatted with two party officials. Wearing an elegant black dress and pearls, Elizabeth stood dutifully by his side.

"We should go rescue my mother," Rick whispered in her ear and Ashley smiled and nodded.

They approached the table and though Rick's mother's smile widened as they grew closer, Rick's father's eyes narrowed and his smile turned into a frown.

The second they were within hearing range, Ben said, "What's this?"

"What's what?" Rick asked, leaning over to kiss his mother.

Mayor Capriotti motioned between Rick and Ashley. "This?" he demanded and Ashley suddenly wondered if the basis for most of Rick's concern about gossip over their relationship wasn't the entire population of Calhoun Corners, but his dad.

She quickly said, "Rick agreed tonight to work with me once my father retires officially."

Happily surprised, Elizabeth said, "Oh that's great!"

But Ben's frown deepened. "As what?"

Ashley again jumped in before Rick could. "I don't want to run the whole darned farm, Ben. I like the breeding end." She smiled prettily and squeezed Ben's forearm affectionately. "And I have enough money that I don't have to do the work I don't want to do."

Ben laughed. "Sorry, Ashley. I just wanted to make sure Rick knew what he was doing."

"Come on, now, Ben," Ashley scolded affectionately. "Would my dad hire somebody who didn't know what he was doing?"

"Absolutely not!" Elizabeth said.

Ben shook his head, looking repentant. "You know what? I'm sorry. I'm tense because of this election and I'm taking everything too damned personally. I'm thrilled that you hired Rick. I know Rick learned a lot the years he was away. I admit I'm having trouble seeing him as an adult." He turned to Rick. "I'm sorry. The timing of your coming home was bad or I would have told you the day you returned that I know you've done some great things and I'm proud of you."

Ashley turned to Rick with a smile, pleased that his dad had been so honest. But though Rick was smiling, the emotion of it didn't reach his eyes. His beautiful blue orbs held an expression of wariness.

Still, he slapped his dad on the back and said, "Don't worry about it."

Ashley waited until they were on the dance floor to ask Rick about his dad and Rick paused, not quite sure what to say. He didn't mind that she'd asked. The problem was that he wanted to tell her. He liked having someone who understood him, especially somebody so pretty, funny and smart. He wanted everything she wanted. The itching of his palm against the soft skin of Ashley's back was a reminder of just how much he wanted it. But any day, any week, any year Senator

Martin could discover his granddaughter and change the entire course of Rick's life.

"At first he seemed angry with you, then he did a complete turnaround."

Rick took a quiet breath. Though it might not be wise to get any more emotionally involved than they already were, conversation might be the only way to get his mind off how physically close they were. "He was furious that I took up with Jen Martin."

"Really?"

"He knew nothing good would come of it and he was right. She hurt me. When I came home, he was sympathetic, but in an I-told-you-so sort of way. I can't even imagine how he'll react when he finds out about Ruthie."

Rather than share his concerns, Ashley shrugged. "He might fall instantly in love the way everybody else does when they see your beautiful daughter."

"Maybe. But he'll also know as well as I do that this situation isn't ever going to be easy. Until I prove myself to be a good parent, a good provider, technically a completely changed person from the guy who created Ruthie, Senator Martin can't find out about her or I'll lose a custody fight. When I tell my dad about Ruthie, he'll wonder if I can keep everything together that long."

"Really?"

Rick shook his head. "He thinks I'm a screw-up because I was. He was angry with me when I dropped out of college, skeptical when I reenrolled to finish my degree after Jen dumped me, and somewhat appeased when your dad gave me the job. But Ruthie will change everything. I'll be back to square one with him."

"I don't know, Rick," Ashley said thoughtfully. "He really seemed to be trying. You saw the way he pulled back and the way he apologized."

"Only because he's not allowed to get angry. It's not good for his heart. For the first time in his life he has no choice but to accept the things his kids do."

"I see."

Rick laughed. "I don't think you do. He rode my back for my entire life, now he's got to accept me. But the truth is I'd be much happier if he'd leave me alone."

She gave him a wide-eyed look of surprise and Rick laughed. "You're always trying to get your dad's attention, so I know it seems weird to you that I've been running from mine. But it's true. Half the reason Jericho and I rebelled was because our dad was so strict. We got in trouble because he dogged us. You got in trouble because your dad let you alone." He laughed again. "We're a pair."

She looked up at him with a soft, feminine smile that just about knocked his socks off. "I think we are."

With that she shifted closer, nestling against him like a lover, not a boss, and everything inside of Rick wanted to lean into her and enjoy her. But he didn't. He couldn't.

"And though I agree with you that Senator Martin *could* try for custody if he finds your baby, I don't think he's ever going to find her since he has no reason to look."

"He might not have to look," Rick said with a laugh. "Jen or her mother could tell him."

"But why?"

"I don't think either would do it deliberately, but it could slip out in an argument."

Ashley shook her head. "Honestly, Rick. I know you see a credible threat. But I don't. I think needing to hide Ruthie is a safety net for you. A logical way to keep you from having to get involved again."

"With you?" he asked, unconsciously pulling her closer. He'd never wanted anything as much as he wanted what she was offering. Not sex. But easy companionship. He'd never spoken so candidly or so easily with anybody. It was almost laughable that she seemed to think he was making up a crisis to avoid her.

"With me."

"Whether you understand it or not, even without my problems with Ruthie, I still wouldn't pursue you. Not to protect myself, but to protect you. I won't let you get so starry-eyed that you miss out on what you need."

"I need you."

"You need somebody in your own social circle. You need somebody who's going to bring you up, not pull you down."

"You do that."

"I might be able to do that for you emotionally, but I can't do it for you professionally."

"You're already teaching me. And I've already hired you. Rick—" She pulled back and caught his gaze. "We complement each other. I've never met anybody who understood me the way you do. I've never met anybody who has helped me and at the same time forced me to be strong, the way you have. You think I need somebody from my social circle but I'd rather have somebody I like." She caught his gaze. "Some-body I trust."

"You trust me?"

She smiled. "If you're telling me I can't, that means you think it's inevitable that you're going to hurt me."

"Only if I leave."

"And what if you don't? What if you spend Ruthie's entire life until she's eighteen living in that guesthouse? Won't we both be sorry if we don't take the gift life seems to have given us?"

Looking into her soft green eyes, while holding her so intimately, he could almost see the future she was de-scribing, and for the first time since Jen left him, he felt normal. Whole. Like a guy who could finally forget his past and move on into a life that was a great deal more than worry over Ruthie.

She snuggled against his shoulder again. "Every decision doesn't have to be made tonight. Let's just enjoy ourselves."

He didn't necessarily agree that they should enjoy themselves, but he did relax with her. Particularly in the car, feeling the quiet companionship they so easily shared. They did fit. And if she was right about Senator Martin never discovering Ruthie then maybe she was also right in thinking that he was using his daughter to keep him from a relationship. If he could make Ashley happy and she could make him happy, everything else shouldn't count, but for some reason or another even when he took Ruthie out of the equation he still had a horrible sense of unease about getting involved with her.

For as much as he wanted it, something in the back

of his mind told him to avoid it at all cost, but without a valid reason for that nagging doubt, Rick had to admit maybe Ashley was right. Maybe all his protests about having a relationship with her were nothing but fear.

Chapter Nine

On election day, the vote count was running so far in Rick's father's favor that within an hour of the seven o'clock closing of the polls it had easily become apparent that incumbent Ben Capriotti had beaten Auggie Malloy. Knowing that the people of the town supported him, Rick's dad was in fine form at the victory celebration being held in his living room, happily shaking hands, pouring drinks, swapping jokes.

Paused in the foyer, watching the scene with Ruthie on his arm, Rick wasn't a hundred percent sure how Ashley had gotten herself invited, but when he walked into the house Ashley was standing in the circle of breeders, congratulating Rick's dad, discussing the future. It struck Rick again how far she'd come in the past few weeks. How different she was. How ready she was to take over and his heart swelled with something he didn't even want to try to identify. He remembered his thoughts driving home from the dinner Saturday night and wondered again if he wasn't manufacturing problems because he was afraid. She seemed so perfect and he liked her so much. But nothing had ever been easy for him. Still, was it so farfetched to think that finding Ashley, falling in love and making a commitment could be as simple as letting nature take its course?

Rick's dad suddenly turned his attention in Rick's direction and Rick watched his father's eyes cloud with confusion when he saw the baby on Rick's arm. Excusing himself from the circle, he walked over to Rick.

"What's this?"

Ruthie slapped her grandfather with her rattle.

"This is my daughter."

Rick's dad's expression shifted several times. Finally he said, "Nobody told me you had gotten married."

"I didn't."

"Then I think you and I need to go someplace quiet to talk."

His father led him to the den at the end of the corridor to the right. The second they were alone in the room, he reached for Ruthie.

"My goodness," he breathed. "She's beautiful."

Rick laughed uneasily. "You're only saying that because she looks like our side of the family."

"I think we'd better say thank God about that. If she looked like Jen Martin it wouldn't be so easy to keep secret who her mother is. Since she looks like us, things will go easier."

Rick nodded. He knew his father would understand that Ruthie's mother's identity would have to be kept a secret.

Further confirming his comprehension of the situation, Rick's dad said, "You didn't tell me about her because of the election."

"Because we were afraid this news would add to the stress of the election."

"Okay." He paused and caught Rick's gaze. "What are you planning to tell people about her?"

"That her mother and I never married."

"And what if somebody asks who her mother is?"

"I'm just going to say she's a girl I met on the rodeo circuit, because that's true."

"I see."

From his father's first comments Rick had thought this was going to be simple, but just as he believed about most of life, nothing was ever easy. Knowing his father would want to dissect every facet of his decision and that he would have to defend himself, Rick took a breath and jumped in with both feet.

"I don't think you do see—"

"No, Rick, you're wrong. I see. A see a guy who is taking care of things." He laughed. "My God. I have a granddaughter."

Totally confused that he'd misinterpreted the situation, Rick said, "You're okay with this?"

"Would it matter if I wasn't? Rick, you're a grown man. Just as I said at the preelection dinner, I might have been having trouble seeing you as an adult when you first came home, but I'm forcing myself and it's getting easier."

"I might end up embarrassing you if Senator Martin finds out about her and files for custody."

Ben shook his head. "I'm not worried. I'll remind people you are an adult, entitled to your own life and decisions. But I don't think there's going to be a problem with Senator Martin. Now that the election is over, even if he finds out about Ruthie, he doesn't have a reason to storm the gates so to speak and take her from you. In fact, it works to his advantage to keep this low-key."

Rick cautiously said, "That's my thought, too."

His dad took a breath. "I can't believe this. This has been some year. I won the election that Mark Fegan worked so hard to make me lose, my daughter married a guy I actually like and I have a granddaughter." He kissed Ruthie's head. She rewarded him with a swat of her rattle. "She's feisty."

"Are you sure you're okay?"

Rick's father laughed. "A man doesn't stare death in the face like I did last year when I had my heart attack without seeing his life for what it really is." He took a long breath and caught Rick's gaze. "I was hard on you when you were younger. I was hard on Jericho, too, but I was harder on you."

Rick laughed. "I was worse than Jericho."

"That's a matter of perspective. But it's all water under the bridge now. You're adults and you both turned out okay. There's no reason for me to ride you. Even less reason to bring up the past."

Rick only stared at his dad. This was more than a civil, normal conversation. His dad had just totally absolved his past.

"Did you know your brother's a detective with the Las Vegas Police Department?"

Unable to stop his reaction, Rick hooted with laughter. "Are you kidding?"

"Nope," Ben said, then slapped Rick's back as he directed him to the door of the den. "And I've decided to offer him the job here in Calhoun Corners, when Chief Nelson retires."

"Chief Nelson is retiring?"

"Life goes on, Rick." He chucked Ruthie under the chin. "Sometimes in the most unexpected ways. I'm glad you're home. I'm glad you're the man you are."

Overcome with emotion, Rick stopped walking and faced his dad. "Thanks."

"You're welcome." He gave Ruthie back to Rick. "She's just a little heavy for me, but stay close. I like to look at her."

Ashley knew she could have been knocked over with a feather when she saw Rick and his dad walking up the hall from the den to return to the party. Not only was the air around them totally relaxed, but also Rick was holding Ruthie.

After giving Rick time to speak with his sister, hand off Ruthie to his mother and mingle with some of the other farm owners, she sidled up to him by the punch bowl.

"Everything okay?"

Rick took a breath, then faced her. "Yeah. Things are good. Really good. My dad thinks you're right about Senator Martin."

"That he has no reason to come after Ruthie?"

Rick nodded. "He's also totally smitten with Ruthie and proud of me."

Ashley let all that soak in, then she grinned. "Well, what do you know."

Rick caught her gaze. "Yeah. What do you know."

Ashley turned away, not about to remind him that roadblocks to their relationship were falling away so fast he shouldn't have any more doubts. She'd said her piece the night of the preelection dinner. She'd given him time to think about it. These decisions were his.

Of course, it wouldn't hurt to remind him she was still interested.

"So," she said, then licked her suddenly dry lips. "Who's keeping Ruthie tonight?"

Touching her forearm, Rick brought her gaze back to his and said, "Me. But now that my dad knows about her, there will be grandma sleepovers in her future."

Holding the gaze of his stunning blue eyes, Ashley said, "Really?"

"Not this week. Maybe not even next, but soon."

"Okay."

"But only if you're sure."

She had never been more sure about anything in her life. Still, she'd come to her conclusions about loving him over a week ago. She'd had time for all this to settle in. Rick had not.

So, she continued to allow him his space, knowing that with their sexual chemistry it wouldn't be a long space.

"I'll be ready when you are."

* * *

When the big black Cadillac began crawling down the lane for Seven Hills on Friday afternoon, everybody stopped working.

Ashley followed the gazes of her workers who seemed hypnotized and she laughed. "You guys have seen visitors before," she said as she turned to walk up to the house. Whoever it was, the style and color of the car hinted that they weren't the type of people who would meet her in the barn. She also decided there was no need to disturb Rick about this until she got past the preliminaries of finding out what they wanted.

She jogged up the back porch steps, glad she'd implemented her more professional policy. Wearing a brown tweed blazer over plain beige trousers, she was appropriately dressed to do the public relations work she was undoubtedly about to do.

In the laundry room, she took off her barn flats and slid into a pair of pumps. As she walked through the kitchen, the front doorbell rang.

"Coming!" she called, hastening her steps to the foyer. She took a breath, pasted on a professional smile and grabbed the doorknob to admit her guest. When she saw Senator Paul Martin standing on her front porch, her smile faded.

"Ms. Meljac?"

"Yes, I'm Ashley Meljac, Senator Martin."

He smiled. "I see you know me."

"Anybody in the United States who watches the news knows you."

"I'm looking for Rick Capriotti."

Ashley stepped out onto the front porch, closing her door behind her. "I figured that out, too. He lives in my guesthouse."

"With my granddaughter."

Ashley swallowed, unsure of what to say. She wasn't the only person who had been convinced Senator Martin wouldn't have reason to look for his granddaughter when the election was over. But it appeared she and anybody else who had advised Rick not to worry had been wrong.

But before she could speak, Rick walked up to the porch. One of the hands had probably told him about the Caddy.

"What do you want, Senator?"

"You and I need to talk."

Rick inclined his head and motioned for the senator to follow him and Ashley quickly said, "You can use my office."

Rather than turn toward the access road that led to the guesthouse Rick changed directions and faced the porch again. "That's probably a good idea."

Ashley opened the door. The senator followed her inside and Rick was right behind him. "The office is back this way," she said, leading the way, but Rick grabbed her arm.

"Sorry, Ash."

He caught her gaze and Ashley's heart stopped. He didn't want her in the room with him. Either he didn't trust her or he didn't consider her as big a part of his life as she considered him part of hers. Still, she nodded slightly and even managed something of a smile.

* * *

Rick hated that he couldn't ask Ashley into the meeting with him, but he knew he couldn't. He had no idea why the senator had come and he couldn't risk what he would say. He walked back the long corridor and directed Senator Martin to take a seat on the brown leather sofa. But rather than sit on the corresponding chair, Rick walked behind the desk and fell into the office chair. If there was one thing Senator Martin understood it was a position of power. For once, Rick had one. And he intended to use it.

"So you work here?"

Rick inclined his head.

"As..."

"Right now, I'm training Ashley to run Seven Hills. Her dad will be home in February and knowing Gene Meljac the way I do he'll test her. If he feels she's ready to run the place, she'll take over as farm manager."

"Then you'll be out of a job."

"As handy as that would be for you, no. I won't be out of a job. Ashley doesn't want to run the place herself. She wants to handle the breeding end."

"Isn't that nearly everything?"

Rick laughed. "Hardly. There will be plenty of work for me to do."

"At a decent salary?"

"Yes."

"And probably romancing Ms. Meljac?"

Rick stiffened, very glad he hadn't slept with Ashley on election night because now they were getting down to the nitty-gritty. If Senator Martin was looking for dirt, Rick wasn't going to provide it.

* * *

Ashley threw a pot of coffee together, then paced her kitchen waiting for it to brew. Though she had intended to fulfill Rick's wishes and stay out of his private conversation, she couldn't do it. She loved him and that meant anything that concerned him concerned her. But even more than that, his feelings for her were so fragile she couldn't let that windbag senator say or do anything that might ruin all the progress she'd made since Rick's arrival at Seven Hills.

Finally the coffeemaker groaned, indicating that it had sucked the last drops of water from the reservoir and Ashley raced to grab her good china cups and saucers and pour the coffee into a pretty silver pot. She arranged the tray, and hurried back to her dad's den.

To her surprise the senator was gone when she entered. Rick sat staring out the wall of windows behind the desk. Ashley licked her suddenly dry lips, then said, "Are you okay?"

He swiveled the chair toward her. "Yeah."

She set the tray on the desk and walked around to where he sat. "No matter what he said, Rick. We can fight him."

Rick caught her hand and before Ashley knew what was happening she found herself on his lap.

"We don't need to fight him."

This close to him, Ashley felt dizzy. Disoriented. She damned near tossed decorum out the window and demanded he tell her what was going on so they could get the discussion out of the way and she could enjoy this.

Instead she caught his gaze. Bad idea. The dizzy feeling intensified.

"He doesn't want Ruthie."

She swallowed. "He doesn't?"

"Nope. He's also got a contingency plan in case Jen tries to use Ruthie as a way to embarrass him. He wants nothing to do with this situation. All he wants is for it to stay quiet."

"So he's set?"

"The only thing he didn't have was my promise that I wouldn't extort money from him."

Ashley nearly bounded off his lap with fury, but Rick wouldn't let her. So she settled for yelling, "How dare he!"

To her surprise Rick laughed. "Luckily I didn't react that way," he said, then smoothed his hand across her hair. "Your hair is very soft."

She slapped his shoulder. "Damn it! Tell me how this ends!"

"I gave him my promise. He wanted me to sign a paper. I told him there was no need. My word was good."

Ashley's breath caught. "And what did he say?"

"He stood up, said, your word had better be good because I'm telling you, Mr. Capriotti, I won't hesitate to use every ounce of power at my disposal to destroy you if you try to destroy me."

"And…" Ashley yelped so frustrated she could have slapped him again.

"And I said, 'then we'll be okay because I don't want you in my life or Ruthie's life. So you go back to being a senator and let me raise my daughter.' He nodded, said, 'Fine,' and left."

Ashley felt her mouth fall open in surprise. "So that's it?"

Rick said, "It appears." Then he pulled her to him and kissed her.

Ashley's breath froze in her lungs.

Rick broke the kiss and for a few seconds they simply stared at each other. This was it. Every roadblock was now out of their way. The could be friends, lovers, anything they wanted to be.

Finally Rick said, "You know we have to get back to work."

She nodded.

"But I'm coming back tonight."

She swallowed. It was a promise and a warning. She knew what he wanted and if she wasn't ready, he was telling her to let him know now.

Holding the gaze of his liquid blue eyes, Ashley smiled and said, "I'll make dinner."

Standing on the front porch of Ashley's massive home, Rick experienced a horrible case of second thoughts. He had flowers because they'd never really dated and he'd certainly never courted her. He'd convinced himself he'd thought everything through, but standing on the wide front porch of the enormous house that belonged to a two-thousand-acre farm, Rick knew he hadn't. He'd forgotten the most important thing of all.

Ashley was rich.

If they were really falling in love, he would want to marry her and if he married her he would eventually be half owner of Seven Hills. Of course, he could force her to sign a prenuptial agreement that precluded him from actually owning the farm because he didn't want her possessions. He only wanted her. And it was as important that she know that as it was for him to demonstrate it.

The prenuptial agreement made so much sense that Rick nearly relaxed, until he realized that no matter how many agreements they signed, if they married he would still be responsible for this farm. For his share of the work, for Ashley being able to do her part.

Of course, he'd already assumed that burden by agreeing to work for her. So, technically, that was handled too.

So why the hell did he feel so damned nervous?

She opened the door and Rick quickly turned. Just as quickly his breath caught. Wearing a sparkly green dress with thin straps that made her green eyes sharp and sexy, with a winking diamond at her throat and her hair tumbling around her in sexy disarray, she was without a doubt the most beautiful woman in the world.

That was why he was nervous.

She smiled. "I made you dinner."

Dinner. He'd forgotten all about dinner. He'd been so nervous about coming over here tonight as a gentleman caller rather than the other half of the team they were creating to run the farm that he'd forgotten she was cooking for them.

She caught his hand and tugged. "Come in."

He shook his head. "Sorry. This is a little new to me."

He stepped inside and she closed the door behind him.

"It's a little new to me, too."

He handed her the flowers and she smiled. "Nobody has ever brought me flowers."

"Really?"

"I was a party girl. I met guys in dance clubs or when I was out with friends." She shrugged. "It's not a very structured love life."

"I know."

Their eyes met. In another life, she had been Jen. In another life, he had been Thad.

She turned and marched down the corridor toward the kitchen to get a vase. "Things are different now. *We're* different now."

"You're so sure?"

She laughed. "You have a child and I have a farm. If nothing else, we're different out of necessity."

He leaned on the counter, enjoying watching her putter around the pretty southwest-theme kitchen. "Yeah."

"Why don't you pour us some wine?"

"Good idea," he said, seeing the bottle and glasses on the counter.

"Better yet, take the bottle and glasses into the dining room and I'll be right behind you with the chicken. I hope you don't mind, but I'm a mashed potatoes and gravy girl."

He smiled. "Sounds good to me."

They ate their dinner in a room lit with candles and smelling faintly of her cologne. Because they worked together and shared the same love of horses, conversation never even lagged. With every second that passed, Rick became more comfortable. They stacked dishes in the dishwasher, took a second bottle of wine to the living room and sat on the lush auburn sofa talking until the room suddenly got quiet. Rick realized he'd long ago set his wineglass on the low table in front of them and Ashley's glass now sat beside his.

He turned and smiled at her. She returned his smile, then said, "This is nice."

"Yeah. Very normal."

She laughed lightly, but Rick didn't see anything funny about the situation. He caught her by the shoulders and leaned to her as he pulled her to him, so he could kiss her.

The second his lips met hers he felt the surge of desire he always felt but this time it was seasoned with a sense of rightness so strong he wondered how he could have missed it before this. He brushed his lips over hers testing the feeling only to realize that he was face-to-face with his destiny. He was about to be everything he'd ever dreamed he would be. Successful. Happy. Totally committed to somebody who was perfect for him.

A landslide of mistakes he had made in his youth poured into his brain, even as the rest of his body became totally obsessed with loving her. He kissed her frantically. She kissed him back with the same energy. He smoothed his hands over her back. She ran her hands down his. With a slight nudge he sent her sliding down on the sofa, but the barrage of mistakes burst in his brain again and he stopped and pulled her up again.

"We can't do this."

She stared at him. "Are you kidding? I think we most certainly can do this, and do it damned well."

He laughed, caught her hand and kissed her knuckles. "I don't mean we *can't*. I mean we shouldn't. Once my dad absolved me of all my past sins, I could look at them more objectively and I realized I made damned near every mistake I made because I rushed." He caught her gaze. "This time, I don't want to rush."

She whispered, "Okay."

He leaned forward and placed a soft kiss on her mouth. "So I'm going to go now before I lose all this good common sense I have."

He rose from the sofa and she rose with him. "I'll see you tomorrow."

He left her standing in her foyer looking totally mesmerized, and walking out to his pickup he squeezed his eyes shut. She was beautiful and perfect for him and he was walking away because for some reason or another he wasn't ready. The worst of it was his excuse of not wanting to rush into this was only half true. He wasn't a hundred percent sure why he was holding back and until he figured out what was going on he couldn't make any kind of commitment.

He just hoped he wasn't making a big mistake by forcing them to wait.

Chapter Ten

Rick woke the next morning to the sound of Ruthie crying and his cell phone ringing. He rolled out of bed, grabbed the phone and answered on his way across the hall to Ruthie's bedroom.

"Hello."

"Hey, Rick. It's Toby. I know it's your day off but it's the day off for lots of people, which means I don't have anybody to send to town for a part for the tractor."

"Not a problem," Rick said, angling the phone between his ear and shoulder so he could lift crying Ruthie out of the crib.

On the other end of the phone, Toby cursed. "Sorry. I forgot about the babe."

"Again, Toby, not a problem." Whether he and Ashley married or not, this was his life. He had a child and he needed a job. Sometimes they would overlap.

"Besides, now that everybody knows about Ruthie, I can just take her with me."

Toby laughed. "That you can."

"Have you called Bert?"

"Yep. He's got the part. It's probably in a bag by now and Seven Hills's account has already been charged."

Rick laughed. "Call him back and tell him I'll be by to pick it up in half an hour. I know he likes to close early on Saturdays."

"Will do."

They disconnected the call and Rick quickly bathed Ruthie, fed her some cereal and dressed her in a warm one-piece outfit that looked like pajamas. He put a sweater on over the pajamalike thing and a hat over her wisp of black hair because, though the sun was shining, it was a cold November day.

After jumping into jeans, a T-shirt and boots, he bundled Ruthie in her travel seat and ran out to his truck. As he'd promised, he was at the hardware store in thirty minutes.

"Well, I'll be damned," Bert said as Rick entered the store, Ruthie at his side in her baby carrier. "I had heard a rumor that you had a little girl."

"I didn't think it would take long for the news to get out."

Rick set the baby carrier on the counter and Bert chuckled. "Yeah, it's out, but the rumor does not do her justice. She's adorable!"

"Thanks."

Bert reached below the counter and pulled out a bag,

then he grimaced. "This is a little heavy. How about if I carry it to the truck for you?"

"It's already charged to the account?"

Bert grinned. "Easiest part of my transactions is to put your purchases onto your bill."

"Great," Rick said, lifting Ruthie from the counter and turning to walk toward the door. "Then let's go."

Bert scrambled behind him. "Yeah, that baby's a cutie all right and I also heard she's Senator Martin's granddaughter."

Rick stopped. "What?"

"I heard she's Senator Paul Martin's granddaughter."

"How did you hear that?"

Bert batted a hand. "Rick, don't be such a spoilsport! Gossip is gossip. Things get around."

Rick took a breath. "Right." He'd never promised Senator Martin that Ruthie's parentage wouldn't get out, only that he himself wouldn't use it. Still, it made him nervous, antsy, to realize he wasn't going to be able to control this situation as neatly as he believed.

"And it isn't like you haven't been through this before."

No. It wasn't. And here was the attitude Rick had been expecting all along. He knew eventually people would connect Ruthie to his misspent youth. He was ready for anything Bert could dish out.

"In fact, this looks like one of your better plans to me. Not only did you get to sleep with a hot babe but also you got your meal ticket." He tickled Ruthie under the chin.

Because calling Ruthie a meal ticket went about eight steps beyond connecting Ruthie to his misspent youth, Rick stiffened. "Excuse me?"

"Oh, come on," Bert said, aghast, as if he thought Rick was playing stupid. "You might not have exactly planned to get Jen Martin pregnant, but once you did you had to realize her granddaddy would pay big bucks to keep this little girl a secret."

Anger surged through Rick. "We're not keeping her a secret." They weren't keeping Ruthie a secret. They were trying to downplay her *mother's* identity, but thanks to people like Bert that particular strategy would have to be amended to Senator Martin's contingency plan.

"Right. And you're not going to hit the senator up for money…at the very least child support."

The anger that Rick had controlled came back about six times stronger. Still, he calmed himself before he said, "I don't want his money."

Bert laughed. "Oh, Rick. You're a con artist. You've always been a con artist. You can play good daddy to Senator Martin if you want, but the people in Calhoun Corners know your games. You can't pretend with us."

Rick set Ruthie's baby carrier on the counter behind him, swung around and hit Bert so fast, even he didn't realize what he was going to do.

"You son of a…" Bert sputtered, blood spurting from his nose.

"Don't ever accuse me of that again."

"Oh, yeah. Tough guy. I remember that now, too." He pivoted and ran behind the desk. "We'll see how tough you are," he said as he dialed 9-1-1. "This is Bert at the hardware. I've been assaulted by Rick Capriotti. I need the police and an ambulance."

* * *

It took about an hour for the news to get back to the farm that Rick had been arrested. With Toby on her heels, Ashley ran to the house and back to the den for privacy when she called. But Rick wasn't permitted to come to the phone and when Ashley sweet-talked old Chief Nelson into letting Rick take just one call, Rick refused to speak to her. She was on her way out the door but Toby stopped her.

"No man wants a woman to rescue him."

She turned from the front door with a sigh. "Are you kidding me?"

"No. And I'm going to warn you of something else. He's gonna be angry when he gets back."

"And I should do what? Let him rant and rave?"

Toby shrugged. "I don't know. Rick hasn't been around in years. He came back changed. I would have never guessed he'd resort to his old tricks of punching somebody, but Bert's a pain in a butt and he also lost a girlfriend to Rick. I'd say this had been brewing for Bert for a while."

"And I should just shrug it off?"

"I don't know. I just know it's not a good idea for you to go to that jail. Give the guy his pride."

So Ashley stayed at the farm. She didn't make any more calls. She didn't drive into town—not even when she realized she didn't have a potato to make herself a baked potato for dinner. Tia called to let her know that the mayor and his wife had gone into town to rescue Ruthie and get Rick out of jail. The sun went down. The moon came up. And Ashley lost patience.

Pulling on a winter jacket to stave off the cold November air, she ran out her front door, jogged down the steps and began walking to the guesthouse. She wouldn't take her car. She didn't want to alert Rick that she was coming and have him lock his door or something ridiculous like that. Plus, she also needed time to plan what she would say.

When she finally reached the guesthouse, she remembered what Toby had told her about letting Rick have his pride and she realized this had always been about pride. He wanted the job. He wanted his privacy. He wanted the chance to raise his own child. He simply wanted what other people got naturally, but what he could never seem to get. Respect. Since his first visit into town with Ruthie had resulted in a fistfight, Ashley suddenly saw what Rick had been warning her about all along. The people of Calhoun Corners simply would not let him forget the past.

Her dad would tell her the fight probably meant Rick hadn't changed. Ashley didn't believe that. She knew Rick in a way few people did. He had bared his soul with her, bossed her, planned with her, eaten with her, cared for Ruthie in front of her. She knew he wasn't the same guy. Though in some respects he had the same cocky attitude, his confidence was tempered with maturity. And that meant there was a good reason for that fight.

She took a quiet breath before knocking. Rick came to the door looking tired. At first it appeared as if he wouldn't let her in, but finally he opened the screen door to her.

Realizing he wouldn't be forthcoming with information, Ashley simply said, "What happened?"

"I hit Bert."

"I know that much," Ashley said, tamping down the hurt that he was back to saying as little as he could get by with in their conversations.

"He accused me of having Ruthie so I could get some money."

"Bert? Sweet, nice Bert?"

Leading Ashley back to the kitchen, Rick said, "Sweet, nice Bert has always been my nemesis."

Ashley stopped walking. Though she remembered Toby had said something about Rick stealing one of Bert's girlfriends, the situation didn't quite mesh. "But you defended Bert. When I had my big plan to get some new suppliers, you said we needed to support the people in our town. You even used Bert and the hardware store as your example."

"My mistake."

"No! Not a mistake! The right thing to do."

"Yeah, well, you see how far the right thing got me. First chance he got Bert pushed me and I reacted badly."

Her guess was right. This was about pride. Unfortunately, since he'd reverted to his old behavior the tables had turned and this was no longer about the lack of respect the town had for Rick. Now, he didn't even respect himself. He believed he'd forfeited that right when he punched Bert. Still, if she handled this properly, she could push him beyond this.

"It doesn't matter what people think."

He spun away from the counter. "Really? Is that why you locked yourself up on this farm?"

"I didn't lock myself up here. This is my home. This,"

she said, spreading her arms wide to indicate the farm, "is what I want. It's what you want, too."

He sniffed a laugh. "Great. Even you think I'm here because I want part of what you have."

Even more pieces of the puzzle fell into place for Ashley. Rick wasn't angry that someone had accused him of having Ruthie as a way to get money. He didn't want anything from the senator and he could easily prove it. All he had to do was show people his bank account. But his motives for his relationship with her weren't so easy to prove. If they married, he wouldn't merely live in her house. Half of everything she owned would be his. But she had a way to reassure him about that, too.

"I didn't say you wanted part of what I have. I said that you want a home. You and I want the same thing. That's not conning somebody. That's working together, building a team, learning to trust."

"Right. You're about the only person in town who sees that."

"Why do you care?" she demanded, suddenly weary and desperate because he wasn't responding to her reassurances the way she had expected he would. "I love you. I trust you. Isn't that enough?"

"Enough? It's what I want more than anything."

"So what does it matter what anyone else thinks?"

"It matters because being in love, making a life is more than the romance. There are tough years. There are lean years. What will you do two years from now, when some new woman moves into town and the rumor starts that I flirted with her just because I talked to her?"

"I trust you."

He shook his head. "You make it sound so easy but you don't yet know what it's like to go into town and have everybody snickering behind your back."

Ashley stared at him. "Have you forgotten I lost half my trust fund?"

"All the more reason for you to steer clear of me! If you don't, you'll soon see what real gossip can do. If we marry, you will constantly hear bits and pieces of things I did or was supposed to have done and eventually mistrust will set in. You won't believe that I'm where I say I am. You might even check up on me."

"I would never do that."

"Then, honestly, Ashley," Rick said, combing his fingers through his hair in frustration, "it will be worse. At least if you check you'll know I'm not lying. If you don't check, you'll always wonder."

"You don't have very much faith in me."

"The problem is I do have faith in you. I believe you love me. I believe you love me enough that you'd hold everything in, rather than tell me, so I don't get angry. And that's why I have to leave."

Panic set in then, stiffening Ashley's muscles and freezing her lungs with fear. "You're leaving?"

"Ruthie and I will be out of here tomorrow."

"You're not going to fight?"

"Fight what? Fight who? Don't you get it? This isn't about one person who hates me or even about me proving myself. This is about an attitude, a perception. I will always be Calhoun Corners's bad boy and if you marry me you'll always be Calhoun Corners's loser." Leaning his head back, he took a long breath. "Look, please leave. Okay?"

Flabbergasted by what he had said, Ashley stayed where she was. "You think I'm a loser?"

"I think people will think you're a loser."

She shook her head. "No, Rick, that's what *you* think. Otherwise the notion wouldn't have even popped in your head. You think I'm an easy mark because I fell in love so quickly? Or maybe you think you're so worthless only a loser would love you. Whatever it is, the real bottom line is that you don't think much of me." With that she turned and ran out of the house.

The next morning, Rick came to the barn and left copious instructions with Toby. He didn't come to the house to say goodbye to Ashley and Ashley didn't go to the barn. The next time she saw him, he was driving up the access road to the main highway. She stood by the fence, watching him, tears brimming in her eyes.

"It's what he feels he has to do."

Hearing Toby behind her, Ashley swallowed. "You know, right now, it's ridiculous for me to be worried about him. I should be upset for myself." She faced Toby with a watery smile. "He thinks I'm a loser."

"Nah," Toby said, sliding his arm over her shoulders companionably. "He thinks he's a loser."

"And anybody who loves him is a loser, too."

"Honestly, Ashley, for Rick this is a no-win situation. That's why he's leaving. He's tired of fighting."

Watching Rick's pickup leave her property, Ashley took a long breath. She would cry tonight. She would beat her pillows, kick at least one wall and cry her eyes out. But she wouldn't do any of that in front of the farmhands.

"I guess we've got work to do."

Toby said, "Yep." He began to lead her to the barn, but he stopped suddenly and said, "You'll be fine."

"I know," she said, but she didn't mean it for a second. If Rick thought he was tired of everybody seeing him as an opportunist, he should see how tired she was of people leaving her. It was the one thing she could no longer tolerate and the one thing he should have known. But he didn't. And it proved he was right. He didn't love her.

Because if he did, he would know that he had more than one option for resolving his problem. Even if he genuinely believed he had to move on, he didn't have to move on alone. But it had never even entered his mind to ask her to go with him or even to share his plan. Just as her father had changed his entire life without ever once considering her, Rick had decided to go, not worried that he was leaving her alone. Not considering that there was no turning back. Because there wasn't. It would be a cold, frosty day in hell before she trusted another man. Even him.

Especially him.

Chapter Eleven

Rick drove his pickup down the lane of his parents' farm, telling himself that this time was different. He wasn't leaving forever and for good. Sure, he would make a home elsewhere, but he would come back to his parents' to visit. There was no reason to feel sad over leaving a town that didn't trust him. The logic and common sense of starting over somewhere else, maybe even going back to Tuscarora now that his mother and Tia had taught him to care for Ruthie, made him feel good. Smart. Capable.

And as for the pain in his heart, he did not regret leaving Ashley. He'd trained her. He was leaving her with Toby. Her dad would always be her backup. And she'd find another man. So Ashley was taken care of. What he hadn't resolved was her accusation that he thought she was a loser.

Unfortunately there was no help for that. If he told her he thought she was probably the most wonderful person he had ever met, then she'd convince him to stay and he couldn't. In some ways her believing that he thought so little of her actually worked in her favor. As angry and hurt as she was with him, she wouldn't regret that he was going. She would move on and look for a guy who deserved her. Somebody in her social circle. Somebody who wouldn't drag her into a pit of gossip.

His mother met him on the front porch and immediately took Ruthie from him. "How's my girl?" she crooned, walking into the house.

"Mom, stop. Don't take her inside. We're only here to say goodbye."

His mother turned. "Goodbye?"

"Ruthie and I are moving on. Not only does everybody in town know she's Senator Martin's granddaughter, which means I've more or less broken my promise to the senator, but I want to go somewhere where I can be myself."

As Rick spoke, his father came out to the porch, but Rick didn't stop talking. His story wouldn't be any different for his dad. "The real me. In Calhoun Corners I'm just a bar fight waiting to happen."

"Is that what you think?"

Rick looked his dad in the eye. "Yes. We both know I'm different. We both know I've changed. But I get tired of proving it. In another town I won't have to."

For a few seconds Rick's father said nothing. When he finally spoke it was quietly. "Why do you think your mother and I said nothing when we picked you up yesterday?"

"Too embarrassed?"

Ben shook his head, laughing slightly. "No. We didn't even ask what had happened because we didn't think there was any need for you to explain. We trust you. You don't have to tell us every thirty seconds that you've changed. If you hit Bert, we know there was a good reason."

"He more or less accused me of getting Jen pregnant so I could extort money from the senator."

Elizabeth gasped, but Ben laughed. "You must be very good at this con artist stuff."

"You can tease, Dad, because it's not you constantly being condemned. I can have changed from here to tomorrow and it won't make one damned bit of difference in Calhoun Corners. I'll always be one push away from exploding."

Ben shrugged. "So what?"

"So what?" Rick asked, suddenly incensed. Though he knew his father had also changed, it appeared he hadn't stopped pushing his son. "Do you think I want my daughter to grow up thinking I got her mother pregnant as some kind of con?"

"When the time is right you can explain everything to Ruthie and she'll believe you just as your mother and I do."

"Right. I'm sure my explanation will be very believable after I marry the richest woman in the county."

"Oh, so that's what this is about. Ashley."

Rick took a breath.

"You love her and you're afraid."

"Afraid isn't the word—"

"Sure it is."

Raking his fingers through his hair in frustration, Rick said, "All right, we'll say I am afraid, but wouldn't you be if you were me! She's the biggest catch in the state for a con artist like me. I don't want to hurt her."

"So don't hurt her."

"Dad, you're making me want to punch *you*," Rick said, only half joking. He'd never hit his father, but his father was certainly pushing him, acting as if this were an easy choice or worse as if Rick had an actual say in it.

"You want to know the real reason you punched Bert?" Ben asked, but didn't wait for a reply. "You hit him because the burden of marrying somebody like Ashley is so big that you panicked."

"I never asked her to marry—"

"When the right one comes along, you don't have to state your intentions. It's understood." Ben sighed. "Rick, you didn't hit Bert yesterday because you're a hothead. The way he tells the story, he hardly pushed you before you punched him."

"So you're saying I'm an idiot."

"Nope, I'm saying you were protecting Ashley."

At that Rick laughed.

"You just said you don't want to hurt her, and you know the gossip would hurt her. So before things got too far you did the one thing nobody could argue with. You reverted to your old behavior to prove you haven't changed and to assure that she wouldn't want you anymore."

Rick said nothing and Ben laughed. "I love it when I'm right."

"Yeah, well, even if you are right the damage is done now. I've proved to everybody that when the chips are down I'm still the same old me."

To Rick's complete surprise his father gaped at him as if he were crazy. "Do you think you only get one shot in life?" He shook his head. "Lord, Rick, no wonder you're angry and overcautious. People make mistakes. You will make mistakes. The key to rising above them is having people you trust to go to for advice and people you trust to simply forgive you. People who are happy to walk with you into the future no matter what your past has been."

Rick turned and stared out at the mountain of trees behind him, suddenly understanding what Ashley had been telling him all along. They'd never had to make explanations or excuses for their pasts. They understood each other. What counted to her was the future. Who he could be or would be. Not who he had been.

Rick faced his mother. "Can you watch Ruthie?"

"Yeah," Ben said with a chuckle. "We could keep her all night if you want."

Rick took a breath. "I'm not sure I'm that optimistic."

Rick drove to Seven Hills not knowing what he intended to say to Ashley. More than that, after the way he'd hurt her he couldn't even assume he would be welcome at her house. He hadn't accused her of being a loser, but he'd let her believe that was how he felt. If she were really smart, and he knew she was, she wouldn't want anything to do with him.

He jerked his pickup to a stop in front of the wide front porch of Ashley's house and jogged up the three steps to the front door. He rang the bell and waited, knowing he'd made the biggest mistake in his life and also knowing that it might be the one mistake from which he could not recover.

When he heard the sound of the front door opening, he spun around to see Ashley standing there, a neutral expression on her face. But that worried him even more. If she were angry, he could talk her out of it. But she wasn't angry. She wasn't anything.

He took a quiet breath and said, "I know what I did was wrong."

Careful not to let any expression show on her face, Ashley only stared at him. She wanted to grab him and hug him. She wanted to tell him the things he had said, the way he had panicked was okay, but she couldn't. He'd hurt her too much. And she absolutely wasn't going to let him do it again.

"You know what you did was wrong? That's why you're here?"

"I know you're angry."

"I'm not angry. I'm hurt. But, you know what? I'm getting very good at taking it on the chin because the recovery time this time was a lot shorter. It took me years to get over Thad, about a day to realize my dad needed his own life and about an hour to realize that if you couldn't get over worrying what everybody said or thought then you weren't the right guy for me."

She took a step back, intending to close the door, but Rick said, "I don't care what the town thinks. That was a smoke screen. A cover."

She paused. She shouldn't be interested in what he had to say. She should close the door and let him go, but her heart asked for just one more minute and she couldn't make herself step away.

"My dad thinks that I hit Bert because I was protecting you."

Ashley laughed. "Protecting me?" She paused, shaking her head. "Of course, from the gossip. You let me think you hated it but what you really hated was exposing me to it."

"I can't stand thinking about everything you're going to face once word gets out that we're dating."

"You don't think the women are going to be jealous?" He laughed. "I don't want anybody to be jealous."

"Really? I had intended to sort of enjoy that part of it."

"I'd prefer it if nobody even looked at us twice. Since I know that's not going to happen, what I want is a second chance."

"A second chance?"

"Yeah. A second chance to let you be yourself with me."

"I already can."

"Can I be honest with you?"

"I thought I was letting you be honest with me."

He ran his hand along the back of his neck. "You're right. You've let me be honest, and lots of times I *was* honest, but most times I walked away before I got to my real feelings."

She caught his gaze and he didn't even flinch. He was vulnerable, raw, probably the most honest he'd ever been and if she rejected him now he'd never be this way with anyone again. He'd spend the rest of his life the same way she would spend hers. Alone. She had the opportunity for the perfect punishment. Or the opportunity to prove to him that they could do this. That they could rise above their mistakes.

She opened the door a little wider. "Well, don't walk away this time."

"You're taking me back?"

"Only if you promise never to pull away again."

"That I can promise. But I can't promise that I won't sometimes be grouchy, bossy, a slave driver, a hard core negotiator and maybe even arrogant."

"Gee, you make life with you sound so tempting."

"It should be. Because I'm driven and driven people are winners. And I know you want to be a winner, too."

She laughed.

"You said you wanted me to be honest, so I'm being honest. If we want to, you and I can make Seven Hills the name that's on everybody's lips at Belmont. We can take the world by storm because I've got the knowledge and the confidence, and you've got the farm."

She swallowed. Was he telling her he wanted her for her farm?

"You've also got looks, charm, imagination and guts. Guts enough to marry somebody like me and toss it in the faces of anybody who looks at us twice."

Her gaze jumped to his. "You want to marry me?"

"I didn't think you wanted to live in sin."

"I don't."

"Then come here," he said, opening his arms and Ashley jumped into them. He kissed her and she melted, the way she always did. The way she always would.

He pulled away and smiled at her. "Now we're about to face our next dilemma as a couple."

"What's that?"

"Should we go get Ruthie from my parents… Or spend the next few hours here…alone?"

She grabbed his hand and led him into her home—their home. "Oh, honey, we've got the next eighteen years to spend with Ruthie. The rest of this morning is ours."

* * * * *

This riveting new saga begins with

In the Dark

by national bestselling author

JUDITH ARNOLD

The party at Hotel Marchand is in full swing when the lights suddenly go out. What does head of security Mac Jensen do first? He's torn between two jobs—protecting the guests at the hotel and keeping the woman he loves safe.

A woman to protect. A hotel to secure. And no idea who's determined to harm them.

On Sale June 2006

Page-turning drama…

Exotic, glamorous locations…

Intense emotion and passionate seduction…

Sheikhs, princes and billionaire tycoons…

This summer, may we suggest:

THE SHEIKH'S DISOBEDIENT BRIDE
by Jane Porter
On sale June.

AT THE GREEK TYCOON'S BIDDING
by Cathy Williams
On sale July.

THE ITALIAN MILLIONAIRE'S VIRGIN WIFE
On sale August.

With new titles to choose from every month,
discover a world of romance in our books written
by internationally bestselling authors.

HARLEQUIN *Presents*

It's the ultimate in quality romance!

Available wherever Harlequin books are sold.

www.eHarlequin.com

HPGEN06

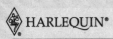

HARLEQUIN®

American ROMANCE®

IS PROUD TO PRESENT A GUEST APPEARANCE BY

QUILL
BOOK
AWARD
WINNING
AUTHOR

NEW YORK TIMES bestselling author

DEBBIE MACOMBER

The Wyoming Kid

The story of an ex–rodeo cowboy,
a schoolteacher and their journey to the altar.

"Best-selling Macomber, with more than
100 romances and women's fiction titles
to her credit, sure has a way of pleasing readers."
—*Booklist* on *Between Friends*

The Wyoming Kid is available from
Harlequin American Romance in July 2006.

COMING NEXT MONTH

#1826 COMING HOME TO THE COWBOY—Patricia Thayer
The Brides of Bella Lucia

Rebecca Valentine might be thriving in the cutthroat world of
New York advertising, but she's losing the battle with her biological
clock. Then her latest assignment takes her to Mitchell Tucker's
ranch. With the cowboy's gentle nudging, Rebecca begins to see
a way to have it all....

#1827 WITH THIS KISS—Susan Meier
The Cupid Campaign

When Rayne Fegan's dad runs afoul of a loan shark and disappears,
she turns to the only man who can help her—her father's nemesis,
Officer Jericho Capriotti. But as their search brings them together,
will their family's feud stand in the way of her happiness?

#1828 NANNY AND THE BEAST—Donna Clayton

The Beast had defeated three of her firm's nannies when owner
Sophia Stanton stepped in to teach him a lesson. Sophia learns
quickly that when Michael Taylor shows fangs, he's really covering
deep wounds. And it isn't long before Sophia realizes that maybe she
is trying too hard to avoid a situation that could be a beauty
with this Beast....

#1829 THE HOMETOWN HERO RETURNS—
Julianna Morris

Luke McCade was gorgeous...*and* the last person Nicki Johansson
wanted to see. No longer the awkward girl from whom he could
steal kisses, Nicki had matured into a gorgeous woman. But could
Luke let go of the past to find a future with her?